Through the gate . . .

Clark started to stand, but it seemed as if the room had begun to spin, picking up speed. Clark felt like he had just chugged a beer after an all-night drinking binge. He felt his stomach turn over. He closed his eyes, but that only made it worse . . .

Lights seemed to come on from everywhere, brightening the interior of the hangar, but especially the fish tank. Langston held up a hand to shield her eyes, leaning her head to the right, trying to plug her ear with her shoulder. Anything to cut the noise level . . .

There was a quiet popping, barely heard over the other noise, like gunfire in the distance. Or maybe firecrackers close by.

The background that had been washed out began to skid into swirling colors. They faded for a moment and then brightened to a near-painful intensity.

Slowly the sound quieted until there was only a low-pitched hum that disappeared. The light faded, and the world outside the fish tank seemed to focus into heavy greens, dark browns, and a few blacks. There was a loud scream from outside like tires on concrete and a rustling as if a thousand birds had suddenly taken flight.

Clark was the first to recover. He stood up, looked beyond the glass, and saw a primeval world of vivid color, with patches of mist rising like steam. Something moved, caught his attention, then disappeared.

"Where in the hell are we?" asked Stepkowski.

Cheney looked around and said, "I don't think this is hell, but I don't know where it is."

"It's not Mars, either," said Clark. "And that's all I really know."

THE EXPLORATION CHRONICLES:
BOOK FOUR

THE EXPLORATION CHRONICLES

THE GATE

KEVIN D. RANDLE

ACE BOOKS, NEW YORK

THE BERKLEY PUBLISHING GROUP
Published by the Penguin Group
Penguin Group (USA) Inc.
375 Hudson Street, New York, New York 10014, USA
Penguin Group (Canada), 90 Eglinton Avenue East, Suite 700, Toronto, Ontario M4P 2Y3, Canada
(a division of Pearson Penguin Canada Inc.)
Penguin Books Ltd., 80 Strand, London WC2R 0RL, England
Penguin Group Ireland, 25 St. Stephen's Green, Dublin 2, Ireland (a division of Penguin Books Ltd.)
Penguin Group (Australia), 250 Camberwell Road, Camberwell, Victoria 3124, Australia
(a division of Pearson Australia Group Pty. Ltd.)
Penguin Books India Pvt. Ltd., 11 Community Centre, Panchsheel Park, New Delhi—110 017, India
Penguin Group (NZ), Cnr. Airborne and Rosedale Roads, Albany, Auckland 1310, New Zealand
(a division of Pearson New Zealand Ltd.)
Penguin Books (South Africa) (Pty.) Ltd., 24 Sturdee Avenue, Rosebank, Johannesburg 2196, South Africa

Penguin Books Ltd., Registered Offices: 80 Strand, London WC2R 0RL, England

This is a work of fiction. Names, characters, places, and incidents either are the product of the author's imagination or are used fictitiously, and any resemblance to actual persons, living or dead, business establishments, events, or locales is entirely coincidental. The publisher does not have any control over and does not assume any responsibility for author or third-party websites or their content.

THE GATE

An Ace Book / published by arrangement with the author

PRINTING HISTORY
Ace edition / May 2006

Copyright © 2006 by Kevin Randle.
Cover art by Edwin Herder.
Cover design by Judith Murello.

ISBN: 0-441-01398-8

ACE
Ace Books are published by The Berkley Publishing Group,
a division of Penguin Group (USA) Inc.,
375 Hudson Street, New York, New York 10014.
ACE and the "A" design are trademarks belonging to Penguin Group (USA) Inc.

PRINTED IN THE UNITED STATES OF AMERICA

10 9 8 7 6 5 4 3 2 1

PROLOGUE

BRIGADIER GENERAL THOMAS HACKETT, WHO had been born on Earth more than two hundred years ago, was still a young man. He was about six feet tall, though the effects of gravity, even the lighter gravity on Mars, had taken its toll. His hair, once dark and thick, was now lighter and thinner. He hadn't gained much weight, but there were the beginnings of jowls on his jaw. He was a study in contrasts.

He sat, looking out onto the Martian landscape that had once been hidden by the domes erected to protect the humans from the harsh environment. Now the weather had been tempered, the highs in the seventies and the lows rarely under forty. The sky was as blue as anything on Earth, and although there was a hint of red in it, as there was in the soil, the tones were changing slightly with the passing time so that they were becoming more Earth-like.

"How long are you going to stare out the window?" asked Sarah Bakker.

She wasn't nearly as old as Hackett. She was just slightly over two hundred, but she didn't look to be forty. In the right light, at the right time of the day, and when she was in a good mood, she looked a decade younger . . . or centuries younger, depending on the perspective.

"As long as it takes," said Hackett.

"Meaning?"

He turned to face her. "Meaning that I feel superfluous here. Meaning that we don't have much to do."

Bakker entered the room and sat down. A century or two earlier, she would have been wearing a one piece coverall, probably in a light blue or green. The coveralls had once been the standard "uniform" for Mars, adopted simply because it was comfortable and it was what everyone wore. Now the styles had changed, as they always did, and they were as varied as anything on Earth. Bakker wore shorts and a long-sleeved shirt. Her knee-high socks had been rolled down to her ankles, and she wore what once were called running shoes.

"We haven't been here all that long," she said.

Hackett looked at her and then back out the window. "There is no way for us to go back."

"No."

Hackett turned and looked at her, happy that she had been able to make the journey with him. At least he hadn't lost her to the experiment. He said, "Remember that UFO guy that we worked with? The one that was sort of the expert on alien life forms and UFO sightings on Earth."

"Sure. Nice fellow with some weird ideas about life in the galaxy."

"Well, he said something to me that always stuck with me, that bothered me. He said, in talking about the stories of a crash of one of those spaceships, that any survivor would be the loneliest creature in the universe. No way to get home and lost among sentient beings that it couldn't understand and who didn't understand it. It would be as lost as it could get."

Bakker felt a chill, not from the room's environmental control. She hugged herself, knowing what would come next, but all she could say was, "Yes?"

"And here we are. Yes, the others are human, but they are so much younger than we are. Their world is one of knowing about alien creatures, faster-than-light travel, other worlds out there, humanity out among the stars. We don't relate to them, and I confess that I don't understand them. They seem, what—superficial? Immature? Self-absorbed?"

"The older generation always believes that about the younger," she said.

"You don't feel it?"

"Tom, what's this about?"

He shrugged. "I'm just feeling out of place. The physics I knew is as out of date as Newton's was when I was growing up. They do things now that I think of as magic."

He turned slightly and pointed at a small square on the wall. Once there might have been a flat-screen hung there, displaying nearly three-dimensional pictures that made it seem as though you were looking out a window. Now it threw a holographic projection into the room so that the viewer was nearly part of the action. There were the odors, the textures, the subtle sounds, of sitting right in the middle of the story. Action going on all around so that it was the full experience and not merely the voyeuristic view that old style television had been.

"I can experience anything I want by sitting right here. Not a simulation but the actual experience with the feelings and substance of the real event."

Bakker looked at Hackett, concern in her eyes. "There something wrong with that?"

"I don't know," he said, "but we—meaning the human race—made progress, gained the stars, because we had to get out to do it. Now we can sit in our apartments and do it. There is no need to get out."

Bakker leaned forward, her elbows on her knees, and said, "There have always been those content to sit at home and not experience anything. And there have always been those who had to know what was on the other side of the hill or those who wondered what would happen if two chemicals were mixed together or who wondered why something was considered impossible."

"When we get too comfortable in a protected environment," said Hackett, "we stagnate."

"Sure and then something comes along to drag us out of our stagnation. Something new or different or just interesting enough for us to notice."

Hackett leaned back in his chair and looked at her, suddenly very happy that he was not as totally alone as that alien stranded on a foreign world would be. He had the one person in all the universe he cared for with him, and she understood him better than anyone else. He grinned.

"So," he said. "How are we going to break out of this stagnation?"

She smiled back at him and asked, coyly, "You mean right now or in the long term?"

"Let's start with right now and worry about the long term a little later."

She stood up and walked to the door. "You coming, or are you planning to use the desk?"

information that had become the files of the Galaxy Exploration Team, and had failed to find adequate answers.

So, he sat in the tiny office that was not reflective of his rank or status, but did provide a clue about the importance of the Galaxy Exploration Team in the modern world, and tried to figure out his next move. No one had suggested anything to him, and he suspected that everyone on Mars would be happier if he had just gone back to Earth like most of the other returnees. Hackett, for some reason, didn't want to do that. He liked living on Mars, even if it had been screwed up by terraforming. Humanity seemed never to be satisfied with the environment it inherited. It always had to improve on the work of nature, regardless of what planet that work was on.

He wondered if the information he wanted was being purposely withheld, but could think of no good reason for it. Besides, everyone he met on Mars seemed to have his best interests at heart. They wanted to help, wanted to give him the answers he sought. But they just didn't seem to have the information at hand and had no real motivation to get it for him. Brigadier generals were a thing of the past, just like the Galaxy Exploration Team and the military.

Every morning, Hackett climbed out of his bed, leaving Bakker asleep, dressed in silence, and then walked to his office. He was there by seven, but no one cared. People rarely visited him. The few who did were those who had come in with him on his faster-than-light ship.

Sitting there, staring at the flat-screen that was really a holographic projection that gave him a window into the world around him, Hackett realized that he was bored. This society seemed to have no sense of urgency about anything. They moved at a pace that was reminiscent of the nineteenth century, not the twenty-third.

There was a quiet tap at his door, but before he could move or call out, the door slid open and a young, doughy man appeared. He was under six feet tall, not really fat, or even overweight. But he just didn't have very good muscle tone. He looked to be a happy man, with no real character to his face, like a happy toddler who had not lost his baby fat. Hackett only knew his first name, which was Bruce. It would be weeks before he learned it was Bruce Pierce.

Without waiting, Pierce slipped into the room, moving to the open chair, in a gait born of a lifetime in the lower gravity of Mars, a semi-waddle that had nothing to do with weight. He grinned broadly.

"How are you settling in?"

He spoke with a slight accent, a pronunciation that was slightly off, but Hackett could understand him if he concentrated on the words.

Hackett looked at him for a moment, unsure of what to say. Finally he said, simply, "Yes."

Bruce cocked his head to one side, as if thinking and then clapped his pudgy hands like a happy baby and said, "Excellent. Then it's time for you to get back to work. Time to produce something for the society that has been so kind to you since your return."

Hackett was suspicious, but then he wasn't familiar with the new Martian society. The one he knew, the one in which he lived, had disappeared two hundred years ago, and all that he knew about interpersonal relations, body language, cooperation, and simply getting along with his fellows was useless now. He knew nothing about these people, other than they seemed happy, they didn't quarrel, didn't fight, and seemed to have no inner fire. But he wasn't sure that was all bad. Sometimes people wasted too much time worrying about others, and sometimes those worries escalated into huge distractions.

He said, "What do you have in mind?"

"Well, we noticed that you've been looking into history, studying the worlds at the time of your departure . . ." He nodded and added, "Not to mention that you lived in that time. A great historical resource for us."

"But everything then was heavily documented, taped, recorded, analyzed, dissected, and archived. What could I possibly add that you don't already have?"

"Perspective," said Pierce. "You understand it from the perspective of someone who was there."

Hackett nodded, understanding that an outsider, no matter how in tune, how observant, how careful, could never really be a part of a society in which he didn't live. He knew from his own experience that reporters traveling with soldiers often thought they understood the soldiers, but they didn't really. You could not understand being a soldier until you were one. A soldier lived in the battle and knew that he couldn't just go home when it suited him like reporters did. A soldier knew that his responsibility was to his fellow soldiers and almost only to those soldiers, not to an obscure theory of journalistic observation or a code of ethics.

So he said carefully, "I'm not sure what I could contribute there."

"Well, then," said Pierce, "what would you like to do? You can't just sit around here. You must do something."

"My training is two hundred years out of date. You have virtually no military force that I can see, and you have stopped exploration of the galaxy," said Hackett. "That sort of leaves a gap in my usefulness."

"There is a military operation, are military operations, on Earth," said Pierce, "if that's what you want to do."

Hackett said nothing. He just shrugged.

"Time dilation has destroyed interstellar flight," said Pierce.

For a moment Hackett was confused, and then he understood. Flights were one way for the crew. They came back to a world they didn't know, as he had. Still, he wasn't sure that the problem should destroy interstellar flight. Maybe there was something for him to do in that arena since he was now an orphan in time.

"I would like to know what happened to the flights that were launched after us," said Hackett. "Maybe design a program that could help us explore the galaxy, at least in the areas around our solar system, without subjecting the crew to the disaster of returning to a world they don't know."

Pierce tented his fingers under his chin and looked as if he was deep in thought. "To what end?"

"I suppose nothing more than my own curiosity and to see something come of our discoveries. Plus, there are some unanswered questions."

"We have traveled to the edges of our system here," said Pierce. "We have no need to go farther, and it is, you might say, a death sentence for the crews."

Hackett nodded, but didn't really like that last part. The crews didn't die while traveling to far star systems. Their families that were left behind aged at a normal rate, matured, and then died. It wasn't quite the same thing, but Hackett understood what Pierce meant and said nothing.

Pierce dropped his hands to the arms of the chair as if preparing to get up. "I suppose that some research in that direction could be very useful to us," he said carefully, as if thinking about it. "At least in the short term." He made no move to leave.

"Then you see some value?" asked Hackett.

"What I see or believe is unimportant here. We all must contribute to the society, especially here where the environment can become hostile so easily. A little historical research might be just the thing."

Hackett looked at the pudgy man and wanted to reach across the desk and smack him. He let the feeling pass and then said, "I'm sure that anything I can learn will be of value to society."

Pierce clapped his hands softly. "Then it's settled," he said. "I'm so glad we had this little chat."

[2]

THE CHAT WITH PIERCE BOTHERED HACKETT because, frankly, he didn't understand it. Martians, as he knew them now, weren't pushy, they had no sense of passing time, and they were loath to be thought of as having a real purpose. They drifted from thing to thing because they could. To live they had to do nothing other than to live. The government provided everything for them at a subsistence level. If they wanted more, and better, then there were ways to earn that, but society didn't really care what an individual did as long as it hurt no one, destroyed nothing, or caused no undue concern.

So, Pierce, showing up suggesting that it was time to

get to work made little sense to Hackett, unless Pierce was attempting to take care of Hackett's need to be useful. Find something that Hackett wanted to do and suggest he do it for some psychological reason.

So, maybe there was something else going on. Hackett turned from his desk and looked at the holographic projector. He touched a button on his desk, and the projector illuminated, displaying the menu in the air in front of him.

He scrolled down, accessed the main library, and then attempted to access the files and programs that related to the first contact with an alien race. Where it had once suggested that access was restricted, the file now opened for him.

Hackett rocked back in his chair, his eyebrows raised in surprise, and searched for anything that would tell him about the aliens.

He clicked on the alien home world and immediately was sitting in the middle of a solar system that was more than two hundred light-years from Earth. It didn't look much like the Earth's system. There were more planets, but there was no evidence of an asteroid belt. There were hints of a single, huge Oort cloud, with some large objects in it, like the planetoids that inhabited a similar cloud around the sun. Closer to the star, in what would be the biosphere, were two planets, one larger than Earth and the other slightly smaller.

The aliens lived on the larger of the planets. Hackett manipulated his way closer, and as he did, he began to feel dizzy. It was as if he was adrift in space with no ship, no craft, floating in toward the alien home. He blinked his eyes and then closed them for a moment.

When the feeling faded, he opened his eyes and found

himself sitting high above the alien world, while it slowly turned below him. He was startled that it looked very Earth-like, with blues of oceans, browns and greens of land, and areas of bright white, a few looking like dirty wool that were clouds. Lightning flashed in some of them.

Slowly he slipped closer, until small features appeared below him. Lakes, rivers, highways, and the urban sprawl of cities that lined the coasts of the oceans and the banks of the rivers but were absent from the centers of the continents. He halted there to study what he was seeing.

If he hadn't been so familiar with the shapes of Earth's continents, he might have thought he was looking down on his home planet. A few of the larger cities were hidden under veils of dirty yellow mixed with brown smudges. In some cases the pollution had spread out over a large area, concealing the finer features.

He saw what might have been small towns, but they didn't have the straight line geometry of Earth towns. More curves and irregular lines were drawn through them, almost as if they had been designed to inhibit easy passage. Maybe they were set up like old European cities had been—to protect against potential invaders.

He slipped closer to the surface, so that now he was seeing the planet as a passenger in an airliner might see the Earth. Fields had been planted in geometric shapes, most likely with cultivated crops, but without the uniformity of those of Earth. He could see no straight lines in those fields, but he noticed a regularity that suggested agriculture.

There were thick ribbons of roads, drawn among the cities and towns, that meandered around as if the shortest distance was somehow abhorrent to these creatures. There was movement of vehicles, but Hackett couldn't tell if they were trucks or single passenger cars, not that it mattered.

He leaned back in his chair, letting the images wash over him, surprised by what he was seeing. There was something reminiscent of Earth about this, though with an alien spin. He had always thought it would be difficult, if not impossible, to understand an alien race, assuming we would have nothing in common with them.

But Hackett realized that wasn't true. These aliens were sentient, just as were the humans of Earth. That was an underlying commonality that meant the aliens' solutions to problems might mirror those solutions found on Earth, and it meant that some of the same problems created by humans on Earth would be created by aliens on their home world.

Hackett chuckled. So much for differences. These aliens had obviously created a civilized society that had advanced to industrialization, which led to various ills of the planet, like pollution.

He wondered if they had wars, then figured that competition for food by their early ancestors would have resulted in fighting that would make them hostile. After all, the prey didn't create the society on Earth, the predator did.

So, humans had studied the alien race, looked at their home world and found them to be like themselves in many respects. That should have scared everyone on Mars and Earth, but it didn't. Hackett wasn't sure but thought that interstellar war might not work for the same reason that interstellar flight didn't work. Time dilation. The attacking side, win or lose, came back to a world that might not understand them and certainly would not want them back.

There was really only one other question . . . well, two. One was whether the aliens had ever approached the Solar System again. That answer seemed to be no.

The second was, what did they look like? The view that Hackett had seen, centuries earlier, was of some kind of intercepted signal that had been digitized, manipulated, and reconstructed. Some had found it valuable to advance political agendas, but Hackett had never thought of it as very interesting.

So now he was about to see the aliens as they really were, based on reconnaissance that was probably about two hundred years old. He brought up the menu again, made his selection, and then sat back.

There were three representatives of the alien race, all looking to be of a single gender, meaning, simply, that any sexual identifiers that might be obvious to other members of the race were not so obvious to Hackett. That was if gender even made any difference to them.

Two were about the same size, and the third was slightly smaller. He thought it could be two males and a female, or two adults and a child, and then he realized that it might be two females and a male, given some of the species on Earth. And then he realized that it might be three different genders, some kind of a family group, or three individuals that didn't really represent much of anything at all.

They were vaguely humanoid, having what looked to be a single head that blended into a neck and torso, which sprouted two arms and two short, stubby legs.

They had faces with what looked like tiny eyes, large ears, and a large nose. It appeared that the mouth was hidden behind a flap of skin, though Hackett didn't know that for certain.

Their hands had long, slender, and flexible fingers that looked like tentacles.

"So that's what they looked like," said Hackett, talking to himself.

Then he laughed as he remembered the long-ago reaction to the idea of aliens. People were frightened of the alien menace, which never came close. They were scared they would die in their beds, killed by alien invaders. Afraid that Earth would be enslaved by the technologically advanced creatures, who hadn't even bothered to return. Even after Hackett and his fellows had gone to the trouble of meeting them at the very edge of the Solar System.

Hackett sat there, watching the aliens rotate slowly about three feet off the floor and two feet in front of his desk. They moved a little, and they seemed to speak, or at least flap their mouths as if speaking, but he heard nothing.

There were other questions he had, but they could wait. He had seen what he wanted to see, learned what he wanted to learn, and wondered why the Martians had withheld the information from him until after his talk with Pierce.

Then he laughed again. He wondered if the Martians believed that he, and Bakker, would react to the alien creatures with hate and fear, as so many of their fellows had two hundred years earlier. Maybe the Martians were just a little bit afraid of him.

He reached out and touched a button, and the display faded away. Nothing left in his office but what had been there earlier.

He pushed himself away from the desk and stood up,

ready to leave. He was a little disappointed in what he had
seen, but didn't know why.

[3]

WHEN HACKETT RETURNED TO HIS LITTLE
apartment, he found it empty. He had wanted to see Bakker
and tell her about his day. He wanted to tell her what he
had learned. He wanted to search for more information
with her, because he found it interesting and exciting and
knew she would be fascinated by it, too. He wanted to tell
her about Pierce and some of his observations, but she
wasn't there.

He sat down on the couch and turned on the television.
Funny how names rarely changed. This new device didn't
resemble the old system at all, but it did bring entertainment into the house like a television, so the name stuck.

At first he tried to access the files he'd seen at the office, but was unable to do it. Instead, his mind wandering
among the stars, he zapped through the various options
available on the home system, and was bombarded by
commercials. He realized he must be getting old, thinking
about the source of names and the way things used to be in
the old days.

Bakker walked in and looked at him. He was sitting on
the couch, surrounded by dancing bears and lions that were
trying to sell him something that "no man could live without." She laughed at the sight.

Hackett waved a hand, his fingers disappearing into the
belly of a lion, and asked, "What's so funny?"

The dancing animals faded. She said, "Commercials. Two hundred years of progress, and we still have stupid commercials trying to sell us crap we don't want or need."

"But they're baby lions," said Hackett.

Bakker walked over and touched a button. The scene vanished, leaving them alone in the room. She looked down at him, blinked, but said nothing.

"Something on your mind?"

"I want to go home."

"You are home," said Hackett.

"No I'm not. I'm on Mars in a society that I don't understand. I want to go home."

Hackett knew immediately what she wanted. She wanted the Mars of two hundred years ago, the way it had been when they launched into space. This was a different world, filled with people they didn't know and a society they didn't understand. He wanted to go home, too, but knew it was impossible.

"Earth, maybe?" he said.

Bakker walked over and dropped onto the couch. She sat near him but didn't touch him. Her eyes were on the floor, staring at the carpeting that was some sort of artificial fiber, resistant to dirt and stains, that could be changed into a variety of colors, depending on the mood and taste of the occupants.

"I wouldn't recognize it," she said.

"No, but we left Earth long before we left Mars on the starflight. We know Earth has changed. Maybe the impact wouldn't be so great. Mars was a new world when we made our flight, but there would be things on Earth that we knew when we left it. Surely some of the things we remember on Earth would still be there and would look the same. The pyramids would be the same."

Bakker took a deep breath and let it out. "It's kind of like dying and then coming back. We get to see the changes, but we can't get back to the life we had before."

"There's no reason to get maudlin. It's more like moving to a new city or country, and then some kind of natural disaster destroys the place you left."

Bakker shrugged as if she agreed but said, "Whatever. We can't go back."

"No, but that's always been a problem. You can never go home. All we can do is make the best of the situation as it stands now."

She didn't like the turn in the conversation. It was as if Hackett didn't want to understand what she was feeling. He had to feel the same way because he was in the same situation. But then, different people—men and women— reacted in different ways.

Hackett said, "I did have a visit from Bruce Pierce today. Wanted to talk about my contribution to society."

"He talked to me, too."

"About?"

"What else? Making a contribution to society. Wanted to know what I was going to do with the rest of my life, now that I had had time to think about it."

"What did you say?"

"I thought I would sell French fries at McDonald's."

"What did he say?"

"He wasn't familiar with either French fries or McDonald's. I found that a little disheartening."

Hackett raised an eyebrow. "I hadn't thought about it, especially since we're on Mars, but then, I haven't seen a

McDonald's on Mars, either. I haven't seen a McDonald's in a very long time."

Bakker moved closer and said, "That's just it. This place is like an alien planet populated by people who seem human, but aren't quite, and who don't know the things we know or care about the things we care about. We're outside the perimeter, with no way to get in."

"Then the answer is simple. We take a vacation on Earth. It shouldn't be much trouble. Not like the old days, when the flights were jam packed and it took weeks to get a reservation and even longer to make the flight."

"How do you know?"

"In two hundred years, with faster-than-light drive, they surely have figured out a way to move between here and Earth in a short time."

She looked at him as if understanding what he was suggesting for the first time. "You serious about this? We can take a vacation on Earth?"

"Why not?" asked Hackett. "It could be fun."

Of course it wouldn't be as easy as he thought, and it would turn out to be anything but fun.

[4]

IT WAS LATE IN THE DAY WHEN PIERCE ENTERED the main conference room and took his seat. He looked first at the window, where the sun sat low on the horizon, looking more like a bright streetlight than the sun. He didn't notice how small it looked, because he had been born on Mars, had never been to Earth, and didn't know how bright the sun could be there.

He turned his attention away from the sun, nodded to his colleagues, and then looked at Nancy Travis, who was currently occupying the seat of leadership.

The chairs, fourteen in all, were arranged around a large circle that was marked on the floor. The holographic projections, when needed for illustration, would manifest inside that circle. The chairs were positioned so that each of the participants in the conference had a front-row seat for the display, and none would be sitting within it.

Behind him was a curved wall painted a pleasing light green. The walls were devoid of decoration, because attention was to be focused either on the other participants, or on the displays in the holo field. There was carpeting under the chairs, but the center of the floor was covered in a light tile. One part of one wall was taken up by a huge window that looked out on the Martian landscape, but the dull, tan curtains were usually drawn so that no one could see out, and sometimes, more importantly, no one could see in.

Travis nodded a greeting at Pierce. She was a small, pudgy woman with a light brown skin that suggested she spent a great deal of time in the sun—though on Mars, a suntan was difficult to maintain. Her skin color was natural and matched, more or less, everyone else's. Hackett and Bakker were exceptions, but, of course, they came from another time.

Seated near Travis was Cheryl Griffin, who was slightly taller and whose straight hair was a light brown. She was older than Travis, and the fingers of one of her hands were twisted with arthritis, a disease that had been nearly eradicated more than a century earlier.

Across from her was Tim Gettman, a tall man, with a round face and big eyes. He looked almost like a gingerbread man with light hair that stuck up and ears that stuck out. He was the junior member of the team.

Travis asked, "How did it go?"

"Well, both of them are receptive to integration into our society and are willing to contribute."

Travis nodded slowly and said, "But . . ."

Pierce took a deep breath and closed his eyes momentarily. He looked down, at the tile circle and said, "I detect a . . . restlessness in each of them. The man, Hackett, seemed to be very interested in our attempts at space travel and had questions about what we have learned in the last two hundred years."

"That is to be expected," said Griffin. "You must remember that they both come from a different society. One that pushed forward without thinking of consequences or worrying about the problems their actions might produce."

"It is much more than that," said Pierce. "Hackett wants to reform his Galaxy Exploration Team—"

"He said that?" asked Gettman.

"Not in so many words, but that was the direction he was going. He was concerned that we had not resolved the question of the alien spacefaring race he found, or rather, they found so long ago."

Travis groaned. "Not that again."

Pierce shrugged. "I'm afraid so."

"What do we do?" asked Travis.

Griffin said, "The simplest solution is to create a file about that alien race. Something for Hackett to access that would answer his questions about them. We do know where their home world is and could manufacture some data that would satisfy him. We have enough archival footage to do a credible job."

"That has been done," said Pierce. "I checked the file just before coming here, and he's already been into it."

"That satisfy him?"

Pierce shrugged. "I don't know, but it should. It answers all the questions he should have, and it uses information he already had."

He waited a moment, and when there were no additional comments, said, "The woman, Bakker, said that she wanted to go back to Earth."

"Those were her words?" asked Travis.

"What she said was that she wanted to go home," said Pierce.

Travis leaned forward, her elbows on her knees, and said, "People who have been forced into long-term absences often attempt to recreate the environment they left. They visit old haunts, they attend events they once enjoyed, and they look for some sort of a connection with their past. Bakker is doing that. She's looking for the world that she left two hundred years ago. She's going to fail."

"Well, of course," said Pierce somewhat sarcastically. "But, those sorts of connections are sometimes made, especially when visiting monuments that haven't been altered by time. A trip to Earth wouldn't necessarily be a bad thing. For either of them."

"You recommend that we allow them a return to Earth?" asked Gettman.

"I don't see any harm in it. Let them have their search for their roots, and then put them to work on something constructive when they return," said Pierce.

"Just how is this going to be paid for?" asked Gettman.

"We're lucky they haven't made claims for past pay based on conventional time rather than on time passed relative to them. It might be that they haven't thought of it," said Pierce.

Travis waved a hand as if annoyed. "These monetary discussions are properly brought to Finance, not to me. We can let them worry about the legalities and their fiduciary responsibilities over there."

"So we're going to allow them to remain unproductive for another several weeks, sucking needed revenues from our limited resources," said Gettman.

"They have already made a huge contribution—"

"Bull," said Gettman. "They took off on a flyer that resolved nothing, other than diverting our resources until time dilation stopped the flights. Now, we have another group of people to worry about who are untrained for anything in the modern world. They're as useless as a laptop computer or an oil fat lamp."

"That's unnecessarily harsh," said Griffin.

"It's the truth," said Gettman, "and you know it. I just wish they'd gone back to Earth with their companions."

Travis interrupted. "We're getting off the beam here. Pierce, what is your recommendation?"

"If we still want to make sure they integrate into society willingly, then I believe this trip to Earth is a necessary step. It will prove that their world is gone and they must adjust to ours."

"And if not?"

"Then we take a hardline and tell them it is time to begin to produce something worthwhile."

CHAPTER 2

[1]

BAKKER WAS SO EXCITED THAT SHE HAD been unable to relax at home, had walked around the small apartment a dozen times, checked her baggage almost every time she saw it, and still couldn't sit still. She tried to concentrate on a book, on a nature program, and finally on Hackett, but had been unable to do so. She was nearly vibrating with tension.

She watched Hackett, sitting quietly, watching the parade of words across the screen as he read an old-fashioned book on physics—one that was nearly a hundred years out of date, but about a hundred years advanced beyond anything he had seen before their faster-than-light flight. When she could stand it no longer, she said, "Let's go."

"We don't have to leave for at least another hour," he said without taking his eyes off the screen.

"Well, we don't have to wait until the very last minute do we?"

Smiling, Hackett said, "No, we don't."

"Then let's go."

Hackett shut off the computer and stood up. He grabbed his bag and said, "Okay."

Together they left the apartment, walked down the brightly lighted hallway, and stepped into the elevator. Without a sound, and with almost no feeling of motion, they descended to the first level. They walked into the lobby, an atrium that reached up four stories, which was all glass on one side and polished aluminum on the other. Lights sparkled, reflected in the metal wall. It looked nice, but had no real purpose except on the ground floor, where it provided the entrances. It was form without function.

Once outside, they hesitated, looking for a private ride, but the use of individual taxis had been discouraged for decades. Busses operated, but they too, were falling into disfavor. Distances between various sites were so short that walking was considered to be the best means of transportation. For those who didn't want to walk, moving "slidewalks" would carry them the longer distances but rarely all the way to their destinations.

"I'd rather walk anyway," said Bakker. "It'll burn off the energy."

"We have plenty of time."

They walked out into the late-afternoon dimness. The sun was still high in the sky, but Mars was so much farther from the sun than the Earth that even the brightest days took on the look of a cloudy afternoon. There were no sunglasses available on Mars, because no one needed them, and lights were on most of the time, day or night.

They walked along a greenbelt that was manicured lawn with bushes and trees, modified for the Martian environment. The trees had large, broad leaves, designed to provide surface area to soak up as much sun as possible. With the huge underground oceans discovered so long ago, neither water nor evaporation presented much of a problem. There was plenty of water available for plants that had long enough roots, and pumps brought the water close enough to the surface for those that didn't.

The greenbelts were meandering paths, like roads, that channeled the foot traffic, but use of them was forbidden to wheeled vehicles. There were a few people walking along them, but not as many as Hackett expected. The Martian sedentary life almost required that people stay inside as much as possible and accomplish as much as possible through the computer networks without going outside or interacting on a personal level. A person could live a long life on Mars without even seeing their neighbors. Everything from food to medical services could be delivered by the network. There were many who preferred that lifestyle.

Bakker had to restrain herself as they entered the green zone. She wanted to run. She was vibrating with energy and excitement. Finally, she looked at Hackett and asked, "Aren't you pumped?"

"About?"

"Seeing Earth?"

He shook his head. "I seem to remember an overpopulated planet that was having trouble dealing with the problems that all those people had created."

"Bull," she said.

"I'm just trying to make sure that I'm not disappointed

in Earth when we get there. It's been a long time since we were home."

"Two hundred years for them to solve some of the problems," she said.

"And two hundred years to create new ones that we haven't even thought about."

"There aren't new problems. I looked it all up. I looked at the pictures of the lakes that have been restored to their pristine condition and oceans that are a deep, clean blue, filled with fish and whales."

Hackett tried not to laugh. "People have the same needs that they've always had. People talk a good game, but few ever make the sacrifices necessary. The politicians ride around in their limousines, while condemning housewives for driving their big trucks. Advertisers know how to sell a product."

"To what point?" asked Bakker. "There can't be that big a need to draw tourists to the Earth."

"I just think we shouldn't be surprised if Earth doesn't live up to all the advertising."

Bakker stopped walking and looked at him. "Just what are you saying? You know what Earth is like. You were born there. You lived there."

"I haven't been there for more than two hundred years. Think about the changes that occurred between the time the United States was created and when we left. Two hundred years have passed since then. We really don't know what Earth is going to be like."

Without a word, she began walking again, but some of the excitement was gone. Some of the anxiety had evaporated. She didn't know if it was Hackett's negative attitude or her own fears that she had been lied to. After all, it wouldn't have been the first time that she had been deceived by those with their own private agendas.

[2]

THE ROOM WAS RELATIVELY SMALL, BUT THERE weren't many people in it. They were middle-aged men and women, considering that they were Martians. All were more than eighty years old, but if someone tried to guess their ages, he probably would have missed by fifty years or more. The Martian atmosphere and the considerably reduced sunlight just didn't age the skin as quickly as on Earth.

This was one of the few groups on Mars that had any real power. Most of the committees were ad hoc, meaning that they sort of formed themselves with a specific but voluntary mission in mind. This committee had a larger problem to confront, and it was one that could affect the whole human race. They had a real mission.

The leader of the group, a man nearly a hundred Earth years old, but who looked to be about thirty-five, sat in the large chair in the center. He had the doughy look of a long-time, native Martian. He held a PDA in his left hand, which showed the same display that was slowly rotating in the holo-tank in the middle of the room.

Richard O'Neill was relaxed, though the information he had was quite exciting. It was the best news since the discovery of faster-than-light travel, though he had not personally experienced that.

When his scientists were assembled, filling only half

the chairs, he said without preamble, and with some excitement, "We have solved the problem."

Two of the scientists, a slender man, who was young, compared with the others, and one who looked somewhat older, who was actually wearing a name tag that said, "Jerry," looked confused. The others, another man and two women, didn't seem to react to the news at all and didn't seem in the least bit interested.

"We have opened the gate," said O'Neill.

One of the women, Sally Clinton, who was nearly ninety, with dark hair, a long face, and bright eyes, said, "I'm not sure what you mean."

"Of course you do. We have a gate to Bernard's Star. Or, we believe the gate is to Bernard's Star."

"It worked?" asked William Curry. He was one of the confused men. He rubbed a hand through hair that was prematurely white with just a hint of black in it. He had a large nose and skin that was about two shades darker than the Martian normal. It looked as if he had been trying to get a tan.

"It did. We have sent a rabbit through. All indications are the rabbit survived the trip and is hopping around on the planet's surface."

Clinton said, "I thought that we needed to get a gateway to the far end. Without that, there is no way for us to get back, or to be sure that the trip was a success."

O'Neill nodded. "All true, but we have solved the problem in a very easy way. We opened the gate, sent the retrieval equipment through, and then shut down the gate at our end. It was activated automatically so that we would know that we had a successful transmission. We could have left the gate open and seen what was going on, but we wanted the experiment to work in the worst-case scenario."

"How did we determine the planet had an Earth-like atmosphere?" asked Bryon Davis. He was nearly as old as O'Neill and looked to be about seventy. The years had not been very kind to him.

O'Neill shook his head. He had just announced they had found a way to travel the interstellar distances without the problem of time dilation, a problem that had stumped them for nearly two hundred years, and no one seemed to care. They sat quietly, looking at him, as if expecting something more or as if they had expected the solution all along. They didn't seem to have a sense of urgency about their situation.

"Exploration of this planet was accomplished more than a hundred years ago. It had both plant and animal life but nothing suggesting a sentient life-form. We used it for our experiments for that reason," said O'Neill.

Jerry Hite, the scientist with the name tag, looked somewhat pleased. He sat quietly and watched as the others talked about the experiment. He was one of those who was always in the background, there, but making no real contribution.

"Then we have gained nothing in the way of new information," said Davis.

"We have learned that we can open our wormhole, dump equipment through it, and have that equipment open up a return wormhole. Or we can send equipment through, hold the hole open, and retrieve that equipment after a fixed period of time. That way we have two-way travel, and we can maintain two-way communications with the explorers."

Clinton shook her head. "Why?"

O'Neill sat back in his chair and looked at her. He wanted to use the old standby and say, simply, "Because we can." Instead, he said, somewhat lamely, "The resources of the Solar System are finite."

"Oh, please. That is the same excuse that has been used for centuries. We must move into space because Earth's resources will soon be depleted. We must move into the asteroid belt because it contains all the raw materials we'll ever need. We must tap into the resources of the Oort cloud. The resources of the Solar System are the next thing to infinite."

"Shortsighted," said Jerry.

"Maybe," said Clinton, "but I see no point in expending what we do have for the dream of interstellar travel."

"Priming the pump," said Jerry quickly.

O'Neill broke in, "It does not involve an expenditure of national wealth for us to travel among the stars. The expenditures have already been made. Now is the time to reap the benefits."

"Lives. You're talking about people's lives. You're endangering their lives on theory and untested equipment for some kind of esoteric desire to spread humanity into the galaxy," said Clinton.

O'Neill looked at her and then looked into the eyes of each of the others one by one. He then addressed the whole group. He said, "I'm not talking about drafting anyone. I'm not talking about untested travel. I'm suggesting that we have found a way of creating two-way travel. We have effective two-way travel, posing minimal danger to the explorers."

"To what purpose?" asked Clinton.

"Expand our horizons. Spread the human race throughout the galaxy. To make sure that we have claim to these worlds before someone gets there before us."

Hite looked startled and asked, "Is that a possibility? Are there other intelligent races moving into our section of the galaxy?"

Clinton shook her head, ignoring Hite and said, "There is no need for that. We have everything we need right here, in our system."

"Eventually the sun will burn out."

Clinton laughed. "In what, four billion years? Will humanity still exist? Will it exist in a form that we recognize? Do we need to worry about that here and now and endanger the lives of our citizens?"

There were murmurs from the others assembled. O'Neill didn't know if it was because of the direction the discussion had taken, if they were bored, or if they agreed with Clinton. All he knew for certain was that they had not been briefed on other intelligent life-forms. At least not yet. Their mission was galaxy exploration and not confrontation with alien races.

He said, ignoring the other, secret argument, "We need to move humanity's eggs out of the single-system basket."

"The same argument used when those generation ships were commissioned. What a waste of our resources and wealth! But, even so, there are representatives of humanity now scattered through our portion of the galaxy," said Clinton.

O'Neill looked almost happy. It was as if he had set a trap that Clinton walked into. He said, "Then we can visit those other worlds, and we can establish communications with our outposts. We can ensure their success, and we can visit our children."

"Waste of time and money, not to mention the danger to the people."

"Is that for you to decide?" asked O'Neill.

She waved a hand to indicate the others. "It's for us to decide. And it's for Pierce and Travis to review our recommendations."

"We can't put the whole human race on hold because you believe there might be some danger. The costs now are minimal because we have the system to make it work. It will cost us virtually nothing other than the power needed to generate the appropriate magnetic fields."

Hite interrupted. "Fascinating as all this is, it does not address the real issue."

O'Neill nodded and said, "The real issue here is the success of the latest experiment."

"What has it gained us?" asked Clinton sarcastically.

O'Neill stared at her and said simply, "Why the stars, of course."

"We've heard that before," said Clinton. "It wasn't true then."

[3]

IT WAS A DIM WORLD, WITH A GIGANTIC SUN IN the sky, but one that wasn't very bright. The world was warm, and there were the remnants of life on it. Life that had evolved in a somewhat hostile environment, at least when compared to Earth, but that environment had softened and the life had shifted around.

So it was an old, dying planet in an old and dying system that boasted little that was of interest to human explorers. For scientists, it would be something they hadn't seen. They would have the chance to watch the star fade and the system turn cold and dark.

But the gate that had been opened by the scientists on Mars connected with something real and tangible, and the scientists were delighted with what they had found. It was a world that could support human life with a minimum of life-sustaining equipment. Just a little oxygen, and a human would not have trouble living on the world, if he got used to the nearly permanent twilight and the oppressive humidity.

They had finally succeeded in opening a gate to a world close to Mars in the galactic sense, one that could sustain life. They believed they had succeeded in creating a way of traveling among the stars that didn't require a ship that moved in increments of the speed of light. They had found a way of bending and shaping space to their will so that the traveler could step through the portal just as simply as stepping through a door and find him- or herself on another world light years from home. This was a trip that took seconds for the traveler and the same number of seconds for those living on Mars. Travel between the two sides of the gate was essentially instantaneous.

Now they could move through the galaxy, and even if the gate could only remain open for minutes, they had learned how to duplicate it. They could open another and another and be reasonably assured of hitting the same target, or so they thought, based on their single successful experiment.

What they didn't know was how far the gate could extend into space. They suspected there was a limit to its range, and other galaxies were still too far distant for it to work with them. But even if the range of the gateway was limited to five or six light-years, they could create stepping-stones across the galaxy. At least that is what they hoped.

CHAPTER 3

[1]

BRIGADIER GENERAL THOMAS HACKETT LOOKED out the window of the shuttle and saw a world far below him that seemed to be pristine. The clouds glowed white over the huge expanses of blue that marked the oceans and the browns and greens that outlined the land. It looked pure and colorful and more beautiful than he had remembered it. The only real change was the coastlines. They didn't look quite as they once had. Something had changed subtly. Hackett didn't realize that it was just natural erosion and a slight increase in the depth of the ocean due to global warming of a couple of centuries earlier.

"I wish we were approaching at night," said Bakker.

"Why?"

"Then we could see the cities."

But as she spoke, they crossed through a twilight and

suddenly the planet was dark. To the north, in one of the mid-latitudes a huge storm flashed lightning, creating a glow at the top of the clouds. At the edge of the cloud cover they could see a pool of illumination that looked like brightly colored light spilled on the ground. It was a moment before Hackett figured out what they were seeing.

"I think the northern-most point is Anchorage," said Hackett.

It was a brilliant jewel of light that extended for miles and then abruptly ended on the eastern and western sides but seemed to fade out north and south. To the east was a broad expanse of light gray that changed subtly until it was darker but filled with flashes of brightness. More storms building in the Pacific.

"It's all so beautiful," said Bakker.

They stared down, looking for anything out of the ordinary. They saw a meteor hit the atmosphere, flare brightly, fragment, and then fade away. It reminded Hackett of a dozen holos he'd seen of great battles at the edge of space.

In minutes there were thousands, hundreds of thousands of lights that marked the western coast of the United States. Some glowed brightly, some were diffused through thin layers of clouds, and some seemed like single points of light, though they marked smaller towns and villages.

"We're almost home," said Bakker in anticipation. "Nearly there."

They could feel a buffeting as the shuttle made deep contact with the atmosphere. They were decelerating slowly, dropping speed and burning off altitude. Hackett leaned back in his seat, closed his eyes momentarily, feeling, for the first time, motion sickness. He didn't understand it, because he was a veteran of spaceflight and hadn't been bothered since the first of his training, which was now more than two centuries old.

"You okay?" asked Bakker.

Hackett didn't trust himself to respond. He believed that if he spoke, he would throw up. He felt sweat pop out on his forehead and wished the shaking, minor though it was, would end. He wondered why this was bothering him now.

And then, almost like an airliner that had burst from the storm cloud into the calmer air beyond a front, the shuttle stopped shaking. Hackett took a deep breath and felt, if not well, at least better. The sweat dried rapidly, and he shivered with the sudden cold.

"You feeling okay?" asked Bakker again, concern in her voice. She reached over and touched his forehead.

Hackett opened his eyes and looked at her. He nodded and said, "I'm fine now."

"Did see Texas? Lights all over the place. Just a big bright glob in the middle of the continent." She seemed pleased with her observation.

"Better target for the enemy," he said, not sure why he had said it.

The shuttle slowed even more, and they banked to the left and then back to the right, bleeding off airspeed and lengthening the glide as they shot for a landing in Florida. Hackett had read that the shuttle recovery fields had been built in Florida because the first of the spaceflights had launched from there, including the old Mercury flights.

In a scene that was reminiscent of the late twentieth century, they were told by a light feminine voice to fasten their seat belts and to prepare for landing. The interior lights dimmed, and the angle of the cabin seemed to change as the pilots lined up with the runways for the landing roll.

In minutes they were on the ground, the tires screaming as they suddenly had work to do. It was a system that had been invented for the first shuttle so long ago that Hackett thought they would have designed a better system in the two hundred years since his last flight. This one worked as well as any and was certainly better than a capsule dropping into the ocean, as the first of the Mercury flights had done.

When they rolled to a stop, they were close to the terminal building, which seemed surprisingly dark, until Hackett realized that the windows had been tinted to block the light from the inside. He couldn't see into the interior.

Lights in the shuttle were turned up, and the other passengers stood up, waiting for the hatch to be opened. Hackett sat still. He could see no point in standing in the aisle, but then maybe the other people had something important to do and wanted to get off in a hurry.

As the line began to move, Hackett stood, stepped into the aisle, and moved backward, blocking everyone behind him until Bakker was standing in front of him.

"Isn't this exciting?" she asked over her shoulder, smiling broadly.

Hackett wasn't sure how he felt. He hadn't been on Earth, literally, for centuries. He didn't know what to expect, except that what he had seen so far was not much different than his experiences with airliners before he had gone to Mars. Lights scattered over the darkened continent, storms raging off in the distance, and not much visible from the upper altitudes. It was an airline flight across the continent and not one that began on Mars. A vague feeling of dread spread through him, though he was unable to explain it. Maybe it was a little too much like returning home after a long time.

They left the shuttle, exiting into a walkway that was little more than a twentieth-century Jetway, though there was no hint of Earth's atmosphere in the sealed metal tube. It wasn't hot or muggy as he had expected it to be in Florida, but surprisingly cool. They followed the other passengers out, into the terminal, and for a moment it was as if they had stepped back in time.

[2]

HACKETT WASN'T SURE WHAT BAKKER WANTED to do now that they had finally reached Earth. She had wanted to sightsee, but Hackett didn't know where she wanted to do that. He was sure that she wouldn't want to return to her childhood home, because it would no longer be there. Few of those temporary urban, or suburban areas would exist in the modern world. They were bedroom communities that had been created for the convenience of the workforce, which would shift and move as the employment patterns changed. Like the migration from the city centers in the mid-twentieth century and the return to those urban areas that marked the world a hundred years later.

If she asked him where he wanted to go, he was going to suggest Las Vegas. It had been the popular destination of choice two hundred years earlier, and he was curious about what it would be like now. There had been dire predictions about the fate of the city when the water ran out, and run out it would, according to the prophets of doom, but he had seen nothing to suggest that it had run out yet.

They stepped out of the terminal, into a cool, pleasant night, and again, that surprised him. It was Florida, and it was late summer. It should be hot and humid, but it wasn't. It was cool, and the sky was bright with the stars. He looked around, searching for a red glow that would be Mars, but didn't see it.

Bakker stood at the curb looking for a cab or other ride, just as she would have done two hundred years earlier. Nothing seemed to be moving toward the terminal. Nothing was parked nearby, and no sea of light that would have marked a parking lot was visible. No hints of a monorail, buses, or cabs.

"I don't see any cabs," said Bakker almost unnecessarily.

"Maybe they don't have them anymore," said Hackett.

"Then how do people get from the terminal into town?" she asked.

"Good question," said Hackett. He turned and looked back into the building, or tried to, but couldn't see anything through the tinted glass.

"Obviously," he said, "there has to be a way."

"And the way is back inside?"

Hackett shrugged. He turned and noticed there wasn't a parking lot in sight. All airports, all docks, everywhere had parking lots. They might be small and almost useless, but from anywhere in the terminals or at the ports you could see cars, cabs, buses, and other means of transport. Here, he couldn't see a parking lot, and it wasn't because there were trees or bushes in the way. Then he noticed that, as on Mars, the street wasn't paved with concrete. It was a wide and slightly depressed greenbelt, short grass that looked fresh and neat, as if no one ever walked on it.

"I suddenly feel like an alien," said Bakker. "I don't know how we're supposed to do this."

"Let's go back inside and see what we can learn," said Hackett.

They returned to the baggage claim area and then noticed a sign above a door that said, "Ground Transportation."

Bakker pointed at it.

"I guess."

They walked over and saw what looked like a tunnel leading into the distance. There was nothing to indicate what it was or how it worked. Just an open portal that seemed to lead to a darkened oblivion.

Hackett stepped through, and a slightly feminine voice said, "State destination, please."

"Las Vegas?"

"That is not option. Please state destination."

Hackett looked at Bakker.

She said, "I don't know. Key West?"

"That is not an option. Please limit your request to a hundred-mile radius."

"Orlando," said Hackett.

"Please enter the lighted portal to your left and take the next car."

To the left a golden light appeared that outlined what looked almost like the entrance to a cave. A violet color came from deep inside, and what looked like a wall rose at the far end, but Hackett saw no car or any other mode of transport available. And there was no indication that there would ever be one.

Hackett walked forward anyway, into an area that was more of a grotto than a subway station. Just as he stepped through the portal, a small, rounded vehicle jerked to a stop in front of him. The car was open to the world, except for knee guards in front and two recessed bucket seats.

Hackett stepped back and gestured to Bakker. She moved forward and sat down. "I'm not too excited about this."

When Hackett entered the car, concerned about its flimsy appearance, two short doors seemed to grow out of the bottom, adding a level of protection. An automatic restraint came up from behind them and then down over their heads. It was like being on a roller coaster two hundred years earlier.

"Well, how dangerous could it be?" asked Bakker.

The car jerked once, almost as if grabbing a chain beneath it, but Hackett was sure the thing rode on a magnetic cushion like mass transit on Mars did.

They entered a tunnel that was only a little larger than the car itself. The walls were curved and glowed with a light incandescence that faded away in the distance, telling them that the tunnel was straight. There was no real sensation of speed, because the walls were featureless and there was no wind blowing on them. Had either of them reached out to touch the wall, they would have left a smear of skin and blood.

"We are moving, aren't we?" asked Bakker.

"I have to assume so," said Hackett. He glanced back, over his shoulder, but could see no sign of the station or platform or loading area.

"How long is this going to last?"

Hackett shrugged. If they had been on Mars, he would

have known. There, stations were spread throughout the system so that no trip between them lasted more than ten minutes. But this was Earth, which was heavily populated, and the distances could be much longer. He had no frame of reference to make an intelligent guess.

"I think we're slowing," said Bakker.

Hackett was about to laugh and ask how she knew, but then he noticed the subtle change in the sensations. He saw that the tunnel seemed to be opening up in front of them. He wasn't sure exactly what it was, maybe a change in the brightness, but it seemed that they were approaching something.

There were no signs that he could see. There were no instructions, either verbal or visual. It was as if anyone who entered the tunnel was expected to know how it worked. Then he thought about everyday life. There were no instructions on doors, or in bathrooms, or on refrigerators. Everyone in society understood how they worked. It had to be the same here, although he would have expected some indication of the station they were approaching. No matter how well someone was integrated into society, they wouldn't know, innately, the names of the various stations.

The car came to a stop, and the restraints folded up and out of the way. The doors slipped down, and the lights on the platform brightened.

"We're here?" said Bakker, a question in her voice.

There was a quiet chime, and a voice said, "Orlando. Your stated destination."

"We're here," said Hackett, grinning.

They stepped up, onto a platform that looked like a duplicate of the one they had seen at the terminal. They walked out, into a world that was very different than the one they had seen at the terminal. The closest thing Hackett could compare it to was a mall of the middle twenty-first century, but this one seemed to have four or five dozen levels, rather than two or three. It looked almost as if there was a stretch of highway moving into some of the old-Earth cities, with a variety of business signs glowing on the sidewalks. They were smaller versions of roadside signs, but they were there all the same, announcing restaurants, fast food, lodging, clothing, electronics, and just about everything else a citizen could want or need.

"Okay," said Hackett. "What's your plan now?"

Bakker turned slowly, taking it all in. "Well, we're tourists. What would a tourist do?"

"Since it seems to be late at night, maybe we should find a place to sleep."

"But there are people everywhere," she said. "Maybe we should look for a travel agency."

Hackett shrugged. He wasn't particularly tired and was fairly sure that he would be unable to sleep even if they did find a room. If Earth operated on a twenty-four-hour basis, there was no reason not to continue the trip. He didn't realize what an ordeal that was going to become.

[3]

THEY FOUND AN OPEN TRAVEL OFFICE, BUT THEY couldn't see any people in it. A disembodied voice greeted them enthusiastically and then offered a variety of options and computer terminals.

"If you are an American citizen and traveling in the next two weeks, please use any of the terminals labeled one; if you are an American citizen and traveling in the next six months, please use terminals labeled two; if you are traveling outside the limits of North America, please use terminals labeled three. If you are traveling into Africa, please use terminals labeled four. If you are new to our agency, please begin at the terminals labeled five. If you would like to hear these options again, please stand where you are."

"Could have started by telling us we needed to go to terminal five," said Bakker.

"Where's the fun in that?"

They walked across the carpeted floor, looking at a tall desk that was set more or less in the center in the room and under a spotlight. There were four computer displays on the desk, arranged so that the screens faced in four different directions giving an impression of privacy. As they approached, one screen brightened, almost as if anticipating them.

"I guess we found the agent," said Bakker.

Hackett read the screen, touched it, read it, and touched it again. A third screen appeared, asking for personal information, including his societal registration number. He glanced back at Bakker.

"What in the hell is a societal registration number?"

"The modern social security number?"

He shrugged, figuring that was as good a guess as any. He typed in his social security number.

The screen flickered, as if disapproving, and then flashed the instruction, "Please wait."

Hackett had to laugh. "You know this is going to be really fucked up now. I've done something wrong, but the computer can't tell me what."

"Maybe the societal registration number has more digits than our social security numbers."

"Yeah, but we should be in their database somewhere," said Hackett.

"The computer might not have the resources to track it so far back, and, who knows, the societal registration number might not even be the same as the social security number," said Bakker.

"You told me to use it."

She shrugged. "So sue me."

"Maybe you should try one of the other computers," said Hackett. "See if your luck is better."

"I don't have a societal registration number either. I don't know how many digits it's supposed to have, and I'm sure the databases are linked."

"So now what?"

"We wait."

"How long?" asked Hackett.

"Give the computer a chance here."

Hackett was growing impatient. On Mars the problems were resolved in a minute or so, but this one seemed to be taking a long time. He would have thought that the computers on Earth would be faster and more efficient than those on Mars. Of course, on Earth, there was a much larger population to deal with than on Mars. Maybe that was causing the delay.

The lights in the entire travel agency brightened suddenly, as if the business day were about to begin.

Hackett looked around and saw two men and a woman enter, spread out slightly, and then begin to move toward him and Bakker. They were all dressed in black, down to their boots and gloves, and they all wore leather belts, which looked like some sign of authority. He knew instantly that the three of them were cops and that he and Bakker were the center of attention.

"I don't like the looks of this," he said.

"Looks of what?" asked Bakker.

But then the cops had them surrounded.

CHAPTER 4

[1]

As he had so many other times, Richard O'Neill stood in front of a group of youngsters. Well, he thought of them as youngsters, though the youngest was about twenty in Earth years, and the oldest was no more than twenty-three or -four. It was a mix of men and women, boys and girls, really, who had studied some science, who had studied some survival—though on Mars if you got lost you probably wouldn't survive long, exposed to the conditions beyond the inhabited areas—and who had an adventurous streak. These were youngsters who didn't know what was about to be asked of them, but who were willing to take a chance, because the money was very good and they had signed on for the twenty-week training that was now complete. They'd probably done it simply because it was something different and they were bored with the lives they led at this point.

O'Neill, dressed conservatively—which meant he had sleeves on his tunic and full legs in his trousers—stood at the front of the room and listened as the kids talked among themselves, seeming to ignore him. He studied them for a moment, wondering if they had the intelligence and strength needed to complete the task—which is always the question asked by the older generation. But when the time comes, the youngsters seem to always step up with fresh ideas and the stamina to win.

He had to grin, because it looked as if they were dressed in rags. That was something else he had noticed. The youngsters always wanted to show their skin. Flawless skin that had no scars or wrinkles or major blemishes. O'Neill was proud of the marks on his body. He had earned every one of them.

He listened as they chattered with one another, using a language that was almost English, but that had been altered because of their reliance on computers and Internet connections, which demanded the use of shorthand. O'Neill found it surprising that any of the generations could communicate with one another.

He heard one of the boys say, "Da 'la-ite?"

A girl answered, "Cu bing w Ches."

"T'all?"

"An be fast ate."

O'Neill shook his head. He thought he understood some of it. "Da 'la-ite," might have been a question about what had happened the night before. The girl went dancing with a friend, but he was lost completely by the last.

Finally he said, quietly, in the "social" English of Mars, "If I can have your attention."

When he got little or no response, he said it again and again, until the kids finally seemed to become aware of him and fell silent.

He grinned broadly at them. "Welcome. I know that you're curious about the assignment and about how many of you we'll need to complete our work. Well, don't worry about the job here. We have more than enough work for everyone."

There was a scattering of applause and then a single, loud cheer.

When they fell silent again, O'Neill laughed. "I'm happy to see the enthusiasm."

"We've little else to offer," said a young man.

That brought a laugh from some, but a young woman said, "Wer-art."

"Yes," said O'Neill. "If you weren't smart, you wouldn't be here. And you're all young, too . . . and re-sourceful. You have a lot to offer us."

The young man who had spoken said, smiling, "E noff so so."

The others laughed at O'Neill's questioning expression. The young man said, "Enough of the soft soap."

"Ah."

O'Neill nodded and moved a step closer. He said, look-ing from one face to the next, "I think we have explained to you what we are doing here, or rather, enough to suggest that some of the assignments can be dangerous."

The outspoken young man waved a hand for attention and started to say something. He noticed the confused look on O'Neill's face and switched to social English. "We've gotten all that."

"What is your name?"

"James Clark. Yes, I have two first names, but my middle name is McKenzie, so my last name is in the middle."

There were a couple of chuckles.

O'Neill looked at Clark, studying him. Young, of course, with his hair filled with gel and swept up on top of his head so that it look like a series of short spikes. He had wide-set eyes, a rounded face, a long nose, and a small mouth. His wasn't an unpleasant look.

"Well, Clark," said O'Neill, "we don't want anyone joining our team under false pretenses, which is why you were given the training that you were."

He looked out at the rest of the group to include them in the conversation. "Of the two hundred applications we took in, you are the survivors of the hiring process. The others either quit or were fired as unsuitable for our purposes. In the course of the last part of your training, you might have figured out some of what we expected."

"Planetary exploration," said one of the women.

"Your name?"

"Jenny Langston."

She appeared to be slightly older than some, but probably no more than twenty-four, as measured by Earth years. She was slender and dark, with an elongated face, a slight, but long nose, and big eyes. She seemed to have an innocence about her.

"Well, Jenny, planetary exploration is correct, but there is a catch."

"I thought there would be, since we haven't sent many people out of the Solar System in a hundred years."

O'Neill wondered if it was necessary to explain time dilation to them. Trips at relativistic speeds had one major drawback. Actually there were more, but the one that had hung them up was that time, relative to those on the ground, was different than time relative to those on the spacecraft. On the spacecraft, they were literally traveling through time, moving forward at a different speed, so that a day to someone on the craft might be a decade to those left behind. It wasn't that the crew didn't survive the trip, it was the society that failed. The travelers might not find anyone waiting for them. That was the problem that had stopped interstellar exploration.

He said nothing about that. He just looked at the half dozen youngsters and said, "Well the time has come for us to do it again."

A stocky girl, Elizabeth Munyoz, stared up at him, blinking as if the light in the room was too bright. She had broad shoulders and a heavy jaw but she had big, bright eyes and fine brown hair.

"B nauts?"

"Not exactly," said O'Neill, understanding the shorthand. "You will not be astronauts."

A big, blocky man named Ralph Stepkowski spoke. He had small features that seemed to be pushed together in the center of his face. "You know, that's the same kind of answer that we got all the way through training."

Now O'Neill grinned. "Possibly because, it is only in the last few weeks that we have perfected the means of what we think of as interplanetary travel. We weren't sure that it would work, but we wanted to be prepared."

"Great," said Clark.

O'Neill turned his attention on the two who hadn't spoken, Bekka Cheney and Stephen Novotny. They, too, were young. They might have been twins, because both had dark eyes and dark hair and regular features, though Novotny had a somewhat rougher edge, as seemed appropriate for the male. As far as O'Neill knew, they weren't related.

"Either of you have anything to say?"

Cheney shook her head. "I'm here to listen."

"Then I suppose that the only thing left to say is that I'll expect everyone here in the morning, ready to go to work."

"You mean take off for another world?" asked Clark sarcastically.

"Exactly," said O'Neill, knowing that they wouldn't believe him and knowing that it was entirely true.

[2]

BEKKA CHENEY WAS NOT SURE THAT THIS WAS such a great idea. On Mars, many people just stayed home, connecting with friends through the computer, talking on-line without seeing anyone in person. There were speciality clubs for those who wanted to get out of the house, but most of those were only mildly popular at best, though a little more popular with the younger people than with the older.

Still, people did get out and socialize, and the six of them who had been at the meeting felt the need to stay together, if only for awhile. They would have a couple of drinks, eat some dinner, and then go their separate ways. They'd return to their homes and computer mates before the night was very old.

They had found a small bistro that had muted music,

good service, and few patrons at the moment. They took a table that was in the back, away from the heaters and away from the noise of the others. They ordered a round of beer, because everyone was supposed to like beer, as they had been told by ads for their entire lives, and they ordered appetizers, because they were young enough that they didn't have to worry about the extra calories. Dieting, at the moment, was something they didn't consider. Later in life, as their metabolism changed, they would begin to eat the foods recommended and produced by the nutrition committee of greater Mars.

Clark was the first to break the unspoken agreement not to talk about work. He was staring down at his beer, as if it were a crystal ball and all the answers would soon appear there, and said, using the shorthand speech that they all understood. "Trav suns now," which translated into, "They're really going to start interstellar travel again?"

"Y no?" asked Munyoz.

"More importantly, why?" asked Langston in the more standard English. She grinned and added, "After all, it's not as if we've used up all the resources in the Solar System."

"We're not likely to, either," said Clark. "I doubt that we could. The asteroids have all the raw materials we could ever use, and even if we did, we could expand operations on the moon and probably find a dozen other moons to exploit, and we haven't even begun to talk about the Kuiper belt or the Oort cloud."

Langston picked up something Hackett would have called a French fry, though it wasn't really made from a potato, and it wasn't really fried, and that wasn't what they called it anyway. It was an incredible simulation, which was another reason that no one at the table worried about calories or fat grams or carbohydrates.

"But someday the sun will go out," she said.

"Yeah, like four billion years from now," said Clark. "Nothing we have to worry about, and nothing we have to plan for now. Let someone else do it. Let someone born a billion years from now worry about it."

Cheney looked at Clark and said, "But wouldn't it be nice not to wait until the very last minute? Besides, something else could happen that threatens humanity."

"I don't know what it could be. A planet-killing comet?" asked Clark. "We're living on two planets and a half dozen moons already. Humanity will survive."

Cheney shrugged. "Maybe it's our destiny to populate the galaxy."

"Now that's an idea I can get behind," said Novotny. "Any volunteers to help me begin the population explosion?"

"I think," said Cheney icily, "that we need some sort of catastrophe before we begin to repopulate. You'll just have to wait until then."

Novotny nodded solemnly and said, "Okay, you're out. Anyone else in?"

There was a bark of male laughter but no volunteers. Novonty shook his head, disappointed, and said, "Okay, but don't come crying to me when suddenly we find ourselves having to repopulate the universe. A task, I might add, I'm up for, so to speak."

"If I might jerk the conversation away from your gonads for a moment," said Clark, "I'm wondering why we are suddenly talking about us doing interstellar exploration without, I might add, having been trained in celestial navigation, piloting, engineering, and a couple of dozen other disciplines."

Stepkowski, who had been drinking his beer quietly and eating more than his share of the fries said, "Quite obviously they have trained others for those specific tasks. We're the landing parties."

"Nope," said Cheney. "I don't like that. We're only trained for Earth-like planets and atmospheres. Our training is more like that of a survival school. We don't have geologists or botanists or biologists who will be going with us. It's like someone has already been lost on one of those planets, and we're to go in and get them out."

"But we haven't engaged in interstellar travel for decades," said Clark. "That's what I don't get."

"Well, we're not going to figure it out tonight," said Novotny, hoisting his beer. "Tomorrow we'll find out everything we want to know."

"Yeah," mumbled Cheney. "That's what's got me worried.

[3]

THE NEXT MORNING, ON ORDERS, THEY ASsembled at the entrance to a large building that in another time and on another planet would have been an aircraft hangar.

Standing near what looked like the hangar doors, one of which was pushed back slightly, was O'Neill. He was dressed as he normally did, looking like a throwback to that earlier time. He waited as the youngsters slowly walked across the tarmac toward him, having gotten off the magnetic bus that had arrived only a couple of minutes earlier.

The place had the feel of an abandoned airfield, though there had never been aviation, in the classic sense, on Mars. The atmosphere was too thin to support an airplane, and even with the terraforming completed, the air thinned quickly above one or two hundred feet. Without distant destinations and with the magnetic trains and buses available, there was just no need for aircraft. Surface transportation was as fast as aviation, and on Mars, it was safer.

When the youngsters assembled in front of him, O'Neill said, "Before we enter the chamber, I want each of you to understand that what you are about to see is classified. That means you do not discuss it with anyone outside our organization, and, to be safe, keep the discussions limited to those who you see with you here now."

"Classified?" said Clark. "Why?"

"Because the information is proprietary, and there are corporate entities who would pay a great deal to know what we're doing here and how we're doing it. The equipment reflects a great investment in government capital and scientific training. We want the opportunity to exploit it for the good of humanity. If that is too much to ask, the bus waits over there."

Clark looked down at the tarmac, almost as if he were a child being scolded by a parent. He mumbled, "I can keep a secret."

"Once inside, we'll begin preparations for your first journey."

"You mean the ship is in there?" asked Munyoz.

"Not exactly."

"We'll get a chance to pack?" asked Novotny.

"Don't worry about that. We'll fill in the details as you need them. If everyone is in agreement, let's go inside," he said, turning toward the interior of what they would consider to be the hangar.

O'Neill knew what they expected. They thought there would be a spacecraft inside. Something to take them into orbit where they would see the interstellar ship. They thought they were going to travel, in the conventional sense, through space, but of course they were wrong about that.

O'Neill looked from one face to another as each registered surprise. The hangar looked nearly abandoned, meaning that it was nearly empty. The floor was clean, and the lights along the ceiling arc were all burning brightly. In the center of the building was what looked like a glass and steel fish tank. One thick cable snaked across the floor, looking like a massive old-fashioned power cable — but no one used wire to conduct power anymore. Wire broke, it heated, and it shorted out. Broadcast, especially over short distances in a controlled environment, was a more efficient way of moving electricity from one place to another, except when the distance was very short and the power requirement massive. Even then, broadcast would be more efficient. The cable probably had another function.

"That," said O'Neill pointing happily at the tank, "is the way we're going to see the universe."

"What is it? Some kind of telescope or computer?" asked Novotny.

O'Neill didn't answer. He waved a hand, motioning them all forward, and said, "Let's go take a good look at it."

They walked across the floor which looked like polished concrete but was actually made of some composite material, and stopped near the fish tank. Beyond it, stuck in a corner of the hangar was a brightly lit, glassed-in room where technicians of some kind worked. Only three or four were visible as they moved around behind the glass.

O'Neill lifted a hand to direct attention to the fish tank, which held six chairs and little else. He looked into the faces of the youngsters and said, "This is our path into the rest of the galaxy."

Clark, who had had too much beer the night before, looked more like a senior who was about to take the final without proper preparation, and said, "In there?"

"Of course, in there," and said O'Neill. "What'd you expect? A spaceship?"

"Now that you mention it," said Clark.

O'Neill shook his head as if he was truly disappointed, but then he realized they couldn't have been expected to figure it out. The answer was a little strange.

"Spaceships don't work," said O'Neill. "They involve too many resources and expenditures of too much national wealth. They're really too slow, no matter how fast they are. They set up paradoxes that seem to defeat the purpose of interstellar flight. Even faster-than-light isn't fast enough."

"So we're going to sit in there and do what?" asked Clark. "Remote view?"

"Please, let's not retreat into that discredited research. This is something more. Something physical that can be proven," O'Neill said.

He then opened a hatch on one of the short sides of the tank and stepped back, waving the others through first. After they were all in, he joined them but left the hatch open.

Once the youngsters had found seats, he said, "Today's mission is more of an . . . orientation flight than anything else. It'll give you the feeling of travel and give you a chance to observe a benign environment."

"I don't understand," said Novotny.

"You were trained on equipment similar to what you see in front of you. You were given classes about environments different than what you would find here, on Mars. You were introduced to various effects of spaceflight, as accomplished in ships, and you practiced using the computer programs that we'll be using here. Without knowing it, you made several simulated flights in this . . . uh, craft. What don't you understand?"

Novotny looked around at the computers and equipment and nodded slowly as recognition dawned.

"So what do we have to do?"

O'Neill grinned. "Just sit there. We'll do the rest for you."

[4]

BRUCE PIERCE DIDN'T LIKE SECRET MEETINGS, and he certainly didn't like secrets. He had been raised by a mother and father who believed that openness was the way to build trust and only those who were evil and who had devious intent kept secrets. But he had learned that sometimes it was necessary to keep secrets. It prevented unnecessary hurt, it sometimes advanced causes that were of great benefit to humanity, and sometimes the secret was so enormous and important that there was simply no choice but to keep it.

Now he sat in a very small room with three others—
Nancy Travis, Cheryl Griffin, and Tim Gettman. They
were old Martians, on top of the food chain, which meant
they had gained power over the years and their motives
seemed to be the best. They didn't like secrets, either, but
they all understood that sometimes secrets were necessary.

They were arranged in a circle so that the holographic
display could manifest in the center of the room, about
four feet off the floor. They all had a good view of it as it
slowly rotated. It wasn't that they wanted to see the display, it was simply necessary, in all its horrifying glory.

Although he knew the answer as he watched the orb
slowly rotate above his head, he asked, "We have gotten
confirmation?"

Griffin rocked back in her chair but kept her eyes on the
orb. It was dark, but not completely black. Fire seemed to
flash across the surface, making it look like a star that had
failed to ignite.

"We have confirmation," she said.

"The orbital mechanics are not precisely worked out,
but we can expect an encounter within the next century,"
said Gettman.

"I don't get this," said Pierce.

"What's not to get?" asked Travis sharply. "You've
been given the data and should have reviewed it."

Pierce held up a hand and said, "I did read it. I just don't
understand why this is only now becoming apparent to us."

"No one was looking," snapped Gettman. "That's all in
the briefing package."

Pierce felt himself getting frustrated. He didn't need a
lecture from someone he considered to be his junior, not to

mention someone who was younger. But frustration wasn't helping.

"It's all about Nemesis," said Travis.

"But we don't know that Nemesis is the cause, or was the cause to the mass extinctions."

Gettman said, "I think the evidence is fairly conclusive. We have an unseen companion to the sun, its orbital rate is something on the order of twenty-six million years, and there is evidence in the fossil record and the history of Earth that shows a periodic mass extinction cycle."

Travis touched a button on the arm of her chair because she didn't want to have the discussion again. She let the computer run through its program while Pierce watched it.

Once again, he learned that the orbit of the Sun's unseen and undetected—until three years ago—companion was such that its closest approach coincided with the mass extinctions of life on Earth.

It all started some 600 million years earlier when life in what was known as the Precambrian was nearly extinguished by glaciation. The massive global cooling created a cold, windswept planet that killed the creatures that had adapted to a warm, wet climate.

Then, more than 435 million years ago came the Ordovician Mass Extinction, which killed half of the species alive at the time. Again this was caused by glaciation, which lowered the seas, which in turn wiped out much of the coastal habitats.

The Devonian ended about 360 million years ago, with seventy percent of life on Earth disappearing. Although glaciation was the suspected cause, this time it was ultimately credited to an extraterrestrial source. The Frasnian-Femennian boundary provided evidence of a meteoric impact of such magnitude that a period of "nuclear winter" descended on the planet.

Two hundred, forty-five million years ago, something between 90 and 96 percent of all life ended. And then there was the mass extinction of sixty-five million years ago, when the reign of the dinosaurs ended and the age of the mammals began. Evidence again suggested a meteoric impact, this time in Mexico, with large craters found in the state of Iowa and a couple of other places.

Pierce knew all that, and he didn't see how it affected them now. Humanity was spread throughout the Solar System, with huge colonies on the moon and Mars and smaller outposts in various other places in the system.

Pierce waved a hand, dismissing the images in front of him and said, "Okay, Nemesis could ruin the environment on Earth, but that doesn't affect us here."

"The theory," said Gettman, "is that Nemesis, in its close approach, disturbs the orbits of the objects in the Oort cloud and the Kuiper belt, hurling those objects into the inner reaches of the Solar System to bombard the planets there. Comets, asteroids, and meteors of various sizes, some gigantic, are flung at us. A strike by the larger objects creates the climate changes that kills off species."

"And," added Travis, "such a strike on a world where life was barely hanging on, such as Mars, could kill everything."

"It could change the orbital dynamics of the Solar System," said Griffin.

Pierce took a deep breath and exhaled it. He knew all that, but he thought the stuff about mass extinctions was created from very thin evidence and the chaos created by

Nemesis would probably be only in the outer reaches of the Solar System.

What he said, however, was, "If the orbit is twenty-six million years, why are the mass extinctions scattered so widely over history?"

"Because," said Travis, "those were the most devastating. There have been other, smaller extinctions, and until now, Nemesis was simply a theoretical construct. Since we found it, we have been able to plot its orbit and learn much more."

"Its influence won't be felt for another hundred years in the worst case."

"But when it is, it will begin flinging huge chunks of rock toward the Sun," said Griffin. "We need to be ready. If we have colonies established on other worlds, outside the Solar System, then aid will be available. If we don't, then we're pretty much on our own."

"But we have time," said Pierce.

Griffin grinned and said, "It's not a good idea to wait until the last minute. You never know what might go wrong."

CHAPTER 5

[1]

THE ONLY GOOD THING ABOUT THE ARREST WAS that, at the very least, they got to see some of the countryside outside the mall. The sun had come up, and Hackett was amazed by the deep, vibrant greens, the bright reds and yellows of flowers, and the general clean and pleasant look of the environment. The fact that he was in the back of a police cruiser with small windows that forced him to lean close in an awkward position didn't matter. He was looking out of the window, on Earth, and that was, at the moment, all he cared about.

"So," said Bakker, leaning forward and trying to get the attention of one of the police officers up front. "What is this all about? You have to tell me."

They ignored her.

Hackett said, "You wanted to see the Earth. Now's your chance."

"You're not worried?"

"About what? We've done nothing wrong."

"Which explains why they arrested us," said Bakker.

"Mistake."

"Well, yeah, it's a mistake, but that doesn't mean much, because we're still under arrest, and they're taking us somewhere in their police car."

Hackett grinned to himself and kept his eyes focused on the world outside. He was beginning to see buildings, but not the tall skyscrapers he expected. These were low, two-, three-, or four-story buildings painted in pastels. It gave them a strange and festive look.

"We're coming up to some city," said Hackett.

"Well, whoppee do. I can't tell you how happy that makes me now."

Hackett turned his attention to her. "Just relax. This will get straightened out. Besides, coming to Earth was your idea, so enjoy it."

Bakker sighed heavily. "I know that it will work out, but it's going to be a hassle."

The vehicle slowed, turned a corner, and then drove down a driveway into an underground parking lot. As soon as it came to rest, the doors popped open.

Hackett started to get out, but a voice from somewhere said, "Remain with the vehicle. You will be escorted."

"What would they do if I bolted for the door?" asked Hackett, quietly.

"Probably stun you some way."

Hackett sat back and wondered. Criminals certainly wouldn't obey a disembodied voice if they had escape on their minds. This meant that there was some system in place to ensure compliance or that the nature of his crime was being taken into account . . . though Hackett didn't know what crime he was supposed to have committed.

The transporting police officers remained in the front of the vehicle. A door in the rough, white exterior of the building opened, and a woman, dressed in the black uniform of authority, walked purposely toward them.

When she was near, she said in a commanding voice, "Please exit the vehicle."

Hackett got out, and a moment later Bakker joined him. They waited for further instructions.

The woman turned and said over her shoulder, "Please follow me."

Hackett leaned close to Bakker and said, "Their procedure really stinks."

"No talking, please."

Hackett shrugged and followed the woman to a small elevator car. Inside he could see no sign of surveillance but knew it had to be there. They were now alone with the unarmed woman. It seemed that the authorities had thrown tested police procedures out the window at some point. Why give criminals a chance to escape? He was sure he could overpower the woman, but she seemed unconcerned that she was alone in a confined space with the two arrestees or that her back was turned to them.

A moment later the doors opened into a lobby that looked as if it might be in a hotel. But Hackett could see subtle indications of security. There were no outside doors visible, and the windows were small, letting in light but not providing much in the way of a view outside or a way to escape, should the glass be smashed.

Across the lobby was a single, massive desk that looked to be behind a plate of glass. Sitting there was another woman. She seemed as bored as any official who had overnight duty and didn't want it.

Without a word the first woman left the elevator and started toward the desk. Hackett and Bakker followed.

"Wha'cha go dere, Sandy?" asked the woman behind the desk using the vocabulary of Earth.

"Two attempted travelers, but they had no ID numbers and are unregistered."

"Ha'n't seen ting like tha' in time," she said. "Where'cha get 'em?"

"Barlow's Travel."

"Tey go money?"

"Don't think that's the issue. They're undocumented."

A door to the side of the desk swung open without a sound. The woman behind the desk said, "Go in."

Hackett and Bakker did as they were told. Now they were in a large office that had two desks set in the center of the room, conversation areas scattered around the walls, bright lights, a light charcoal carpet, and a band of brushed aluminum about shoulder high around the walls. Windows stretched along one wall. They were about three feet high and broke the aluminum band. Hackett noticed a series of subtle lines in those windows that were probably reinforcements.

"Doesn't look like any of the precinct houses I've ever seen," said Hackett.

A different woman, this one also dressed in black, but wearing a knee-length skirt and no weapon, came through another door, holding out her hand.

"Hi. I'm Wanda."

Hackett forced a smile and said, "Well, hi Wanda. I'm Tom and this is Sarah. Why are we here?" He noticed that her English was more like what he and Bakker spoke rather than the verbal shorthand used by so many of the people on Mars or the strange dialect that some on Earth used.

"You're undocumented."

"So someone said. What does that mean?"

Wanda waved a hand toward one of the conversation areas. "Why don't we sit down?"

Each of these areas had a short couch, two facing chairs, an end table and a coffee table. Although it wasn't obvious, everything was fastened down so that nothing could be used as a weapon. Hackett took one of the chairs, Bakker the other, and Wanda dropped onto the couch.

"So," she said, "How are you doing?"

Now Bakker spoke up. "I don't mean to be rude, but I'm not really in the mood for small talk. Just what in the *hell* is going on here?"

"Well, let's see," said Wanda pleasantly. She took a PDA from her pocket. "Seems you two were attempting to travel to Las Vegas."

"Yes," said Hackett cautiously.

"You input a societal registration number that was inaccurate. When asked for a confirmation, you repeated the same number. Travel without proper identification is not lawful."

Hackett leaned an elbow on the arm of the chair and then rubbed his face carefully with his hand. He noticed that he needed a shave.

"I'm afraid that we don't know what the societal registration number is."

That surprised Wanda. She crossed her legs slowly and opened her eyes widely. "But everyone has one."

Hackett gestured at Bakker and said, "We don't. We have social security numbers, but they apparently don't have enough digits."

"No one has used the social security number for fifty years. It was replaced."

"Well, then, there you have it," said Hackett. "We'll just need to replace our social security numbers with these new societal registration numbers. Easy as that."

Although he said it, he didn't believe. Once government was involved, nothing was easy.

[2]

"I'M SORRY," SAID WANDA, "BUT NEITHER OF you is in the computer system."

"Have you tried our names?" asked Bakker.

Wanda looked at her as if sickened. She said, "Of course, but without a link to a societal registration number, there is little chance that you'll be in there."

"Okay," said Hackett, "I didn't want to say this, but we should be in the history books. Maybe that'll help to tell you who we are."

Now Wanda gave him a quizzical look. "In the history books? Is that supposed to be some form of identification?"

Hackett looked embarrassed but said, "No. I meant that it would prove that we are who we said we are."

"The history books?"

"Yes."

"The ones we studied in school?"

"Yes."

"Why would you be in the history books? More to the point, *how* would you be?"

Bakker didn't like the turn the conversation had taken but thought it worth a shot. She said, "We were involved in the first of the faster-than-light experiments."

"That was two hundred years ago," said Wanda.

"Yes," said Hackett, sounding like the relieved teacher whose dullest student had finally made the simple connection between two rather obvious points.

"How could you be in the history books?"

"Because we were on that flight," said Bakker.

"I don't remember the names of those people. As I remember, they didn't do much other than break through the speed of light for a couple of seconds."

Bakker nodded and said, "Something that physics of our time had said was impossible until we did it. It should have brought in a new era of spaceflight." She shook her head sadly. "But it didn't."

"And we don't need faster-than-light to travel inside the Solar System."

Hackett realized that they were arguing with someone who didn't understand the implications of what was being said. He wondered how many people would remember the names of Robert Fulton or Wilbur and Orville Wright if he asked them. He wondered if she even knew who Neil Armstrong was, or for that matter anything about the first moon landings.

"Early flights left the Solar System," said Bakker.

"Yes," said Wanda, her forehead wrinkling in thought.

"I heard something about that, but it was a long time ago. Nobody does it anymore."

"Yes," said Bakker, "because of time dilation. We got caught in one of those warps. We were gone from here for nearly two hundred years."

"Impossible. No one lives to be over two hundred. I think some guy lived to a hundred and seventy-five once. They had a thing about him on the television."

Hackett shook his head and realized that it wasn't going to work. She didn't understand who they were and didn't understand they had left Earth before the latest round of registration. He asked, "What do we need to do?"

"I'm afraid there isn't much you can do," said Wanda. "You're not in the computer."

"Well, look, it has to be about the middle of the morning by now," said Hackett. "People are at work. Isn't there someone to call or e-mail?"

"Call or e-mail?" asked Wanda, apparently stumped by the terms.

"Electronic communication?"

"Oh, through the computer system?"

"Yes," said Hackett.

"Won't do any good. Everything that I have is everything that they have. I can link into the main databases from here. If we were to communicate with Washington, they'd just tell me the same thing that I learned here and then ask me why I bothered them with a question I could answer myself."

"Mars?" said Bakker.

"I have all the Martian records."

"Well," said Hackett, "we obviously exist. We are obviously here. We obviously were able to get on a shuttle. So, what is the next step?"

"Our hands are tied," said Wanda. "We know that you came in from Mars. We're going to have to send you back there. It's the only course of action we have."

"Now wait a minute," said Bakker. "We came here as tourists. But both of us were born in the United States. We're citizens."

"Nope," said Wanda shaking her head. "I have no record of that."

"So you're just going to put us on the next flight out of here."

"It's not quite that easy, but yes, that's what's going to happen. In the meantime, you'll have to remain here."

"Here as in this city, or here as in this police station?" asked Hackett.

"Why, here in the station, of course."

CHAPTER 6

[1]

CLARK WASN'T SURE WHAT HE EXPECTED. THE method of travel had not been explained to him fully during his instruction, and he certainly didn't think it would be initiated while he was sitting in what he thought of as a glass-walled conference room. He had expected a full-blown briefing before departing from the conference room to where the ship waited. He didn't get the briefing and, he learned, they would depart while they sat in the conference room.

After giving them a preliminary lecture and telling them the trip would begin soon, O'Neill had backed out of the cage, which he called the fish tank, almost as if expecting one of them to make a break for it. He had been smiling, but it wasn't a pleasant grin.

He had then hurried across the floor to the control booth

and joined the people there. Clark had turned in his seat and watched, somewhat surprised by the behavior. He wasn't sure that he liked anything he saw.

"What's that all about?" asked Cheney. She used the verbal shorthand of her generation, but everyone in the fish tank understood her easily.

"Who knows?"

There was a high-pitched hum, a quiet sound that was barely audible, but that hurt the ears. It slowly increased in volume until it sounded like a banshee shriek. Cheney and Novotny clamped their hands over their ears, but that didn't stop the pain and did little to deaden the sound.

Clark started to stand, but it seemed as if the room had begun to spin, picking up speed. Clark felt like he had just chugged a beer after an all-night drinking binge. He felt his stomach turn over. He closed his eyes, but that only made it worse.

"What the hell?" shouted Langston, trying to be heard over the increasing sound, which now included a roaring like a hurricane.

Lights seemed to come on from everywhere, brightening the interior of the hangar, but especially the fish tank. Langston held up a hand to shield her eyes, leaning her head to the right, trying to plug her ear with her shoulder. Anything to cut the noise level.

Munyoz tried to see beyond the lights, but the hangar had disappeared in the brightness.

"Stop it!" demanded Clark. "Turn this thing off."

But it was too late to shut down.

There was a quiet popping, barely heard over the other noises, like gunfire in the distance. Or maybe firecrackers close by.

The background that had been washed out began to skid into swirling colors. They faded for a moment and then brightened to near painful intensity.

Slowly the sound quieted, until there was only a low-pitched hum that disappeared. The light faded, and the world outside the fish tank seemed to dissolve into heavy greens, dark browns, and a few blacks. There was a loud scream from outside like tires on concrete and a rustling as if a thousand birds had suddenly taken flight.

Clark was the first to recover. He stood up, looked beyond the glass and saw a primeval world of vivid color, with patches of mist rising like steam. Something moved, caught his attention, and then disappeared.

"Where in the hell are we?" asked Stepkowski.

Cheney looked around and said, "I don't think this is hell, but I don't know where it is."

"It's not Mars, either," said Clark. "And that's all I really know."

[2]

INSIDE THE CONTROL BOOTH, WHERE THERE were good heaters and good soundproofing, they heard almost nothing from the outside world. O'Neill could see the fish tank and the atmosphere around it brighten. It looked as if a bank of lights inside had been turned on, all pointing outward. He lost sight of the men and women inside in the glare of the light. A moment later, the light faded and the fish tank was gone.

That hadn't surprised O'Neill. He knew that the whole thing disappeared. He knew that everything in it would disappear. He knew that, after one hour, the process would automatically reverse and the fish tank would reappear right where it had once stood. Anyone inside and anything attached to the outside would come back to the hangar. Any living thing on the outside would probably not survive the trip, though he didn't know that for certain, and he knew of no experiment that had been conducted to learn the answer. He realized that no one had mentioned the possibility of something attaching itself to the exterior of the fish tank before.

"They're gone," he said unnecessarily.

One of the technicians, an older woman named Janice Rankin, with long brown hair and small eyes, kept her eyes on a flat-screen and said, "Landed. Safe. There is movement inside the fish tank."

"How do you know how far they've traveled?" asked O'Neill. That had been explained to him before, but he just couldn't wrap his mind around the concept.

"It's based on power consumption here, length of time for the signal to reach us, and our targeting information," said a male technician, with a hint of arrogance in his voice. He kept his attention focused on the data parading across the screen directly in front of him. It was all color coded, not only for ease of review, but also to add a little snap to the visual.

O'Neill nodded. He had been told that they were folding space in some fashion so that locations that had been hundreds of light-years apart were now closer, just like someone folding a piece of paper. Dots at opposite ends now touched. Travel time was reduced, as were the vast distances. The fish tank and the fields it generated made all that possible and, in theory, allowed them to travel to the stars.

"Where's the visual?" he asked.

The male technician, Richard Mason, pointed at a screen and said, "Right there."

The travelers looked seasick. They were pale, and one of them was doubled over, apparently sick to his stomach. The others were attempting not to watch him retch, trying to regain their own equilibrium.

Beyond them was the world outside the fish tank. It was the first real glimpse O'Neill had had of such a world. The technicians and scientists who had developed the travel method had seen it all before, and O'Neill had seen the holos of those experiments, but he had never been present when the signal was coming in.

"Looks like Earth," he said.

"Of course. We sent them to Earth."

O'Neill stepped back so that he had a better view of the screen. He knew that the process they were now using for travel allowed them to have a real-time view of what the crew inside the fish tank was seeing. He knew that they were still in the fish tank, and he knew they would remain inside it for the next hour. That had been their orders, and he'd locked them in. He had no doubt they could open the lock if they really wanted to, but he suspected on this first trip, they'd be content to look through the glass at the world around them. Besides, they didn't know they were on Earth. They didn't really know where they were.

And, if nothing else, they seemed to be disoriented by the travel process. That alone should keep them in place for part of the time.

He watched the travelers, who now sat still, almost as if

they were in shock. He waited for one of them to speak or to do something, but none of them did. They seemed to be caught up in the situation, almost as if they didn't understand it.

He had hoped, on their first trip, they would have been a little more adventurous, a little more curious about the new world around them. Instead they sat, almost quietly, as if they didn't care they had traveled, nearly instantaneously to a new world. They didn't seem to want to move.

"We've got a spike on the power chart," said Mason.

"What's that mean?" asked O'Neill.

"Only that they have begun to draw a little more power. Probably the air-conditioning."

O'Neill nodded but said nothing. He just wanted the people in the fish tank to do something. Anything.

[3]

CLARK STOOD UP SLOWLY, AS IF HIS BACK WAS sore and his legs hurt him badly. He took a tentative step forward, toward the hatch, but he had no intention of opening it and stepping out. He was just trying to see if he could move without getting sick again.

He looked out, into the jungle around them. He tried to see if there was any animal life and thought he saw the bushes rustling. Having lived on Mars his whole life, where there had never been thick vegetation or winds, he wasn't sure exactly what he was seeing. He understood the concepts of wind, just as a person from a landlocked environment understood the concept of tides and waves, but he had not seen winds blowing hard enough to disturb the environment, and he had not seen so much vegetation, except in pictures.

"There," said Langston, pointing. "Something black or dark, moving around."

Clark saw it, too. A small creature with two arms and two legs that looked like pictures of Earth monkeys that he had seen during training. It was smaller than he thought it should be, and he wondered if it was a juvenile or infant and, if so, where was the adult.

"You're not going out are you?" asked Novotny.

Clark shook his head. "Nope. I just want to get a better look outside."

"We're on Earth," said Langston.

"How do you know?" asked Clark.

"I recognize the trees and that monkey. And I don't believe that evolution on two planets would produce the same species, or species that are so close that I would recognize them easily, so we must be on Earth."

"You sure?" asked Stepkowski.

Langston shrugged. "No, but even if we predict a similar environment, I don't see evolution following exactly the same path. Even on Earth, when a species is isolated, it tends to adapt to its new environment. I mean, there are variations, and the longer the separation, the more varied it becomes, until it evolves into a different animal."

Her voice was clipped, and some of the words were difficult to understand in her verbal shorthand, at least to those listening in from Mars, but most of it was English. Scientific concepts were difficult to discuss without using scientific terminology to describe them, which forced Langston away from the verbal shorthand.

Clark held up a hand like an old-fashioned traffic cop.

"I really don't want or need a lecture on planetary evolution."

"I was merely explaining why I believe that we're on Earth," said Langston.

"I'll go you one better," said Cheney. "We're on Earth in case something goes wrong. They wouldn't fling us to some faraway system, because then they couldn't help us if there was trouble. On Earth they can get help to us in a couple of hours. This trip is designed for us to get our feet wet."

"She's right," said Clark. "We have almost no survival gear, and we didn't get much of a briefing before they sent us out. We're on Earth."

"Then we can open the hatch and step out without worrying about alien creatures or some kind of hostile environment that would kill us," said Langston.

Cheney laughed. "We were born on Mars. These are all alien creatures."

Clark thought about opening the hatch, but didn't, remembering they were not to open the hatch. He said, "There's nothing for us to explore out there."

They sat quietly, most of them over the temporary motion sickness. Clark walked around the interior of the fish tank, inspecting it carefully. He noticed little things that suggested it was stronger than it looked. The glass was very thick but seemed as clear as the finest crystal.

There was no real warning as the retrieval began. Just the beginning of the high-pitched hum. Clark moved to his chair and dropped into it as a brightness flashed in his face. He tried to blink away the spots in front of his eyes, and as his vision cleared, he realized that they were back in the hangar.

He wondered if he could have talked to O'Neill back on Mars from Earth, or if O'Neill could talk to him. He knew there had to be some kind of communications equipment and that the techs could watch what they were doing in the fish tank, but no one had said anything to them about this. Maybe they wanted to see how the crew reacted on a short, relatively safe trip and had only watched them.

There had been no feeling of motion and no indication that they were moving. Only a slight vibration and the deafening sounds. Had the scene outside the fish tank not changed, it would have seemed like they hadn't moved.

They watched as O'Neill crossed the hangar floor. When he reached the hatch, he reached out, his hands covered in thick, apparently rubberized gloves. He unlocked the hatch and opened it, but he didn't step through. At that moment, the exterior of the fish tank was too cold to touch.

[4]

THEY REASSEMBLED IN A CONFERENCE ROOM closer to the city. They had ridden on the magnetic bus, the trip slowed, given the delicate stomachs of some of the passengers, who were still recovering from the trip from Earth.

On one side of the conference room, a banquet was laid out. Hot and cold foods, breads, rolls, and cakes, soft drinks and wine. Something for everyone, even those who were still a little queasy.

O'Neill waited for them all to get something to eat or drink and then sit down. He waited to see if any of them were going to get sick and run from the room before he joined them. Sitting in front of him was a glass of wine and a plate of shrimp.

The shrimp had been grown on a farm on Mars, had been adapted to life in the lighter gravity and to life in water that was not quite as thick as that on Earth. They had to introduce a weight on top of the tanks that forced the water down, creating a greater pressure. Genetic manipulation had created shrimp that thrived in the waters of Mars, but they tasted different than those on Earth. Not necessarily worse, or better, just different.

When everyone was settled, O'Neill said, "A little celebration for your graduation. As of this evening, you are all members of the revitalized Galaxy Exploration Team."

Clark, the most vocal of the members, said, somewhat sarcastically, "Graduation? What in the hell are you talking about?"

"Today's mission, though a real mission, was also your final test." He smiled benignly at them. "It was only to Earth and you deduced that rather rapidly. A journey into a very safe environment."

"Except for the travel," said Langston.

"Not really. No one was injured in the travel. The tank has withstood all environments into which it has been sent, and we have developed a list of planets we wish to visit."

Clark looked at him and asked, "And how many manned voyages have there been?"

"Just the one, but we have had other experiments. All successful. We have sent living creatures through a number of times, all successfully."

Clark took a sip of wine. "I don't wish to sound disrespectful, but what is the purpose of sending us into these environments?"

"That should have been covered in your training," said O'Neill.

"I understand the theory behind it, but not the rationale," said Clark.

"You're splitting a fine hair there," said O'Neill.

Cheney put her glass down and said, "Because, if we're going to have colonists going to those worlds, we have to send someone to make a physical recon. Simple as that."

Clark nodded but didn't seem mollified. "Then let the colonists make the recon."

"You're now an explorer," said O'Neill. "In the traditions of Columbus and Magellan."

"Columbus died broke, and Magellan failed in his attempt to sail around the world," said Clark. "He died a long way away from home."

"His ships made it," said Cheney.

"But he didn't," snapped Clark. "I see no real need for us to make trips. Everything can be done automatically. Everything can be done remotely, without the risk of a single life. What really is going on here?"

"Please," said O'Neill, "I think you miss the point. We now have the opportunity to colonize the galaxy. We can move the human race out of the confines of the Solar System and ensure that it survives through all of eternity. The galaxy can belong to us. The meek will inherit the system, because the rest of us will have gone to the stars."

"Grandiose plans," said Clark, "but really irrelevant to me. Besides, I thought the generation ships we launched two hundred years ago did that. Gave us the stars, not to mention faster-than-light. We already own the stars."

O'Neill suddenly felt tired. These youngsters were being offered a chance to see the galaxy. To go out among the stars without having to sacrifice decades of their lives. They could do in an afternoon what should have taken years. They would have the chance to see worlds that were as different from Mars as Jupiter was. They would see life-forms as strange as those found under the ice on Europa. They would have opportunities to do things that most people only dreamed about, and they would do it in relative safety, yet they seemed not to care.

"I envy you," said O'Neill. "I wanted to go, but the computer models suggested that the young had a much better chance of survival. My bones are old, my joints stiff, and I just can't keep up. You have those gifts, and you wish to sit here, on Mars, and play with your computers."

Clark laughed and then stood up holding his wine glass high. "To us, who will soon see the rest of the galaxy."

CHAPTER 7

[1]

THE JAIL CELL WAS MADE OF A MATERIAL THAT looked and felt like molded plastic and might have been that, but it was stronger than any plastic Hackett had ever seen. It was scratch resistant, paint resistant, and was red. All red. A deep, rich color that was obviously the color of the material used to make the cell and not paint. Hackett didn't know if there was any psychological reason for using red cells. All he knew was that this cell was most definitely red.

There was a molded bunk that had no mattress but was comfortable without it, a molded chair that was part of the floor, just as the bunk was part of the wall. There was a sink that responded to him by spraying water when he stuck his hand under the faucet and that shut off when he moved away from it, and a toilet with a privacy screen.

Since this was a modern facility, there was access to a computer database. He could research the law, as it applied to him, he could read books and magazines online, and he could tap into some of the entertainment programming, so that he could watch if he didn't have the ability to read. There were filters, of course, screening out what would be considered inappropriate, but that was to be expected.

It was not a bad jail cell. It was comfortable, and it had no iron bars. Just a strip around the entrance that had some sort of electrical charge to it. If he stepped over it without permission, he would find himself curled into a ball on the floor, with the electrical impulses from his brain to his muscles scrambled so badly that it would be impossible to stand or fight, let alone flee.

Hackett sat in the chair and looked out into the hallway. They had cleverly put Bakker in a cell that was far enough away that he couldn't see her. He tried to call to her but got no answer. He noticed how quiet it was all over the cell block and realized that the sound was absorbed by the plastic. No rowdy prisoners disturbing their fellows in the night. Just the tranquil jail cell where he could contemplate his transgressions or surf the Internet looking for a legal excuse for his behavior or watch the entertainment provided. If he could have accessed room service, it would have been as comfortable as some of the hotel rooms he had occupied.

A meal was served by a robotic tray, which wheeled itself into his cell, unaffected by the electrified strip in the doorway. Hackett looked down at the food. It didn't look very appetizing. He wasn't sure what it was, only that it had probably been prepared automatically and selected for its nutritional content, not flavor. But he was hungry, so he ate.

When he finished, the robot wheeled itself away. Hackett stretched out on the plastic bunk, his hands under his head, and stared up at the red plastic ceiling. Although he wasn't tired, he felt himself grow drowsy.

He awakened with a start, sensing something in the cell with him. He opened his eyes slowly and turned his head. Another robotic tray, holding his breakfast was standing near his bunk, waiting with the patience of the pyramids. He had slept through the night.

When he finished eating the morning meal, but before the tray could escape, a figure appeared in front of the cell. Hackett stared for a moment and then recognized Wanda.

"Have you finished?" she asked.

"Of course."

"Then please come with me."

Hackett made no move to get up.

"I have work to do."

Hackett grinned broadly. "I'm not sure that I care about that."

"This isn't my fault. You were the one who entered the country illegally."

Hackett leaned back against the plastic wall, which was surprisingly comfortable. "I'm an American citizen, so I should be able to enter the country. In fact, since I am an American citizen, I have committed no crime."

"You can't prove that," said Wanda.

"I'm not sure that's supposed to be a requirement. I was born here . . ." and then he stopped. He had been born more than two hundred years ago.

And then he grinned. "How about I give you my birth date and you run my name?"

"Look, why don't you just accept your fate here? All we're going to do is send you back to Mars. Someone there can straighten this out. It should have been done before you boarded the shuttle to come here."

Hackett looked at his watch and then down at the red plastic floor. He hadn't enjoyed much of the trip to this point. It had been noisy and crowded in the mall. There had been too many people, even late at night. There was too much noise everywhere, except in his cell. But the access to the Internet was limited, and the entertainment was nothing great.

Hackett finally decided that he had screwed around long enough. Whatever the problem was, it wasn't one that Wanda had created. It made no sense to take it out on her. He stood up and walked to the line on the floor that marked the edge of his jail cell.

"You may exit," she said.

As he stepped out into the corridor, Wanda moved off, toward the cell occupied by Bakker. Now he could hear noise. He thought he could hear a generator somewhere, but it could have been something else. And he heard other, quiet sounds—the rattling of a keyboard and the low, quiet voice of someone talking into a voice input for a computer.

And there was a buzz that he couldn't place. Not like a bee or another insect, more like an electric motor or electrical field. It might have been the barriers to the cells, but he hadn't heard the sound when he was in his cell.

Bakker appeared looking more angry than anything. She seemed to be rested and clean but very annoyed.

"They're sending us back to Mars," she said as she got close to him.

"Yes."

"Is that all you have to say?"

Hackett shrugged. "What do you expect? There's nothing I can do about it."

"Well, the least you could do is be annoyed."

Now he smiled. "Yes, but sometimes I just can't even work up the energy for that."

"So, are they going to let us back on Mars?"

Wanda nodded and said, "Yes, they have to take you. It was your point of departure."

Hackett laughed. "I can make a case that the Earth, New Mexico specifically, was my original point of departure, but here you are, about to throw me off the planet talking about original points of departure."

"You do not have the proper documentation," said Wanda patiently. "When you have the documentation, there will be no other issues."

"And we can come back to Earth?" asked Bakker.

"But of course."

Bakker nodded, not knowing that she would return much sooner than she suspected.

[2]

AS THEY WALKED INTO THE MAIN SQUAD ROOM of the police station, they saw Steven Weiss sitting in one of the chairs that lined the wall. He was an older man, having been born on Earth two hundred years earlier. But he hadn't aged as well. Also like them, he had been on the original Galactic Exploration Team. But unlike them, he had left Mars as soon as the faster-than-light mission was over.

Weiss was roly-poly with a shock of hair above his ears, a scraggly comb-over that fooled no one and a pasty complexion that suggested he stayed out of the sun now that he was back on Earth. He had an overcoat folded over his arm and was sitting with his feet flat on the floor and his knees together like a maiden on her very best behavior.

Neither Hackett nor Bakker recognized him as they walked into the room. When they appeared, he stood up and waited quietly.

"Ah, someone to help," said Wanda.

Hackett turned, recognized Weiss, and immediately felt the old emotions. Weiss had not been a trusted member of the team and had often worked for his own benefit, considering the mission and the others on the crew as pawns for his use. He had a habit of working behind the backs of his colleagues.

"What are you doing here?" demanded Hackett.

It was only then that Bakker saw Weiss, and she physically recoiled from him. She didn't say a word, but looked as if she wanted to retreat.

Weiss grinned and advanced, holding out a hand. "I'm here to help you."

"Why, am I suspicious?" asked Hackett.

Wanda asked, "You're from Washington?"

"No, I'm from Colorado, but I found myself in the same boat as these two when I returned to Earth not long ago. My records were old, lost, in disrepair, and almost hopelessly out of date. I have experience in repairing this type of damage."

"What can you do?" asked Hackett.

"Well, I am the precedent. I can cut through the red tape for you."

Bakker studied him carefully and asked, "If there is a precedent, why is everyone so confused here? How come we weren't aware of this on Mars?"

Weiss waved a hand as if to say her questions were meaningless, but answered them anyway. "Because no one expected you to come back to Earth so soon and no one thought to alert the Martian authorities about these identity problems. It was something that would take care of itself eventually."

"Let's find a place to sit down," said Wanda.

They all moved to one of the conference areas near the narrow windows and took seats, with Weiss facing Hackett and Bakker and Wanda off to one side, almost as if she was the referee.

"Okay," said Weiss. "The governmental view of social needs has changed since we left Earth. They are taking a more active role in the development, education, and care of children. With that comes, not a social security number, but a longer societal—"

Hackett held up a hand to stop him. "We know all about that."

"What you don't know is the information coded into the number. Genetic identity for one thing. A health status, based on your genetic identity is included. All of this information is needed to travel because—"

"The government always knows best," said Hackett sarcastically.

"Actually, what this does is keeps people out of certain areas that would be bad for their health. It prevents the spread of communicable diseases and actually keeps those with a certain genetic disposition from ranging too widely and infecting other areas."

"Sounds racially based to me," said Bakker.

"Well, in a sense, but it is best for society as a whole. If you have too many people with a recessive gene that induces certain disease, isn't it better if they don't encounter one another?"

Hackett shook his head, thinking that the argument sounded vaguely familiar, but didn't want to get into a philosophical argument with Weiss about it. Right now he wanted to get out of the police station.

"What do we need to do?" he asked.

"I've cleared the way. Your DNA was taken when you joined the military, and another sample was taken when you were detailed to the that galaxy team you always talked about. Same with Bakker. The genetic records were made then. New records were completed upon our return to Mars, and it has all been reviewed. All that information is available to the various governmental agencies that have an interest in this."

"Is there a point?" asked Bakker.

"Of course." He pulled his PDA out and touched the screen. "I was able, overnight, to access the records and begin the procedure. You both are cleared now and have a new societal registration number."

"What?"

"The purpose here," said Weiss, "is to keep certain genetic codes, certain mutations, certain diseases out of the New World . . ." He laughed at the term *New World*.

"Anyway, nothing was found in your genetic makeup

that would suggest that either of you is a threat to the health safety of the continent . . ."

Hackett stared at him, his mind racing. He understood the implication of what Weiss was saying, even if Weiss didn't get it. Someone had created standards in the form of a genetic code, and if that code was not met, then the individual was deemed *inferior*, even if that wasn't the term used. Their travel was restricted. And if their travel was restricted, what else might also be restricted, all for the overall benefit of society?

If they took that a step further, then a child would have his genetic code examined at birth, and if that code was flawed, what happened to the child? Hackett didn't want to know, but he was certain he knew the answer. They had reached, in part, the brave new world where everyone was perfect, or as perfect as science could make them.

"So we can go?" asked Bakker.

"No," said Wanda, quickly.

"Actually," said Weiss, "yes and no. We need to visit Washington and get some things ironed out there—"

"Why?" asked Hackett. "Isn't everything wired together now? All databases available and everything can be done through the Internet?"

"Yes, but you are required to take certain tests under strict conditions. While all that can be arranged here, it's easier to pop up to Washington and do that this afternoon." He looked at Wanda and added, for her benefit, "They'll be in my custody, so that we can leave here."

"Is this really necessary?" asked Bakker.

"If you want to stay here for any length of time or return to Earth permanently, then, yes it is. If you want to climb back on the shuttle and head to Mars, then no, it's not. You become a Martian problem."

Hackett turned his attention to Bakker. She sat with her head down, staring at the floor. Finally she looked up and said, "This just isn't worth it. I want to go home." This time by home, she meant Mars.

But the truth was that she had realized that her reason for wanting to visit Earth was to connect to her past. With the new rules and regulations, with genetic mapping, and with apparent monitoring of everyone's activities, this was a world she didn't know and had never known. This was not her home—that world was long gone.

"Let's just go home," she said sadly, again.

"When's the soonest we can be off this damned planet?" asked Hackett.

Wanda said, "There is a shuttle on Tuesday."

"And for the next three days, what do we do?" asked Bakker.

"You'll have to stay here until we can put you on the shuttle."

Weiss looked from one to the other and asked, "Are you sure that's what you want?"

"No," said Bakker, "but that's what we're going to do."

[3]

THEY LANDED ON MARS IN THE CONVENTIONAL sense and found themselves in the terminal that looked like the one on Earth, except there were fewer people around, they didn't feel as restricted by the gravity as they had on

Earth, and the air was somehow fresher, cleaner, and not as thick.

And, most importantly, there were no customs agents waiting for them and no officials who wanted to arrest them for being alive and on Mars. Just the same tired lines that they had gone through before as they were checked onto the planet.

As they were walking through the terminal, Richard O'Neill separated himself from the crowd and move toward them. He held out a hand and said, "Welcome home."

Hackett shook the hand first. "How did you know that we were arriving?"

"Checked the manifests of the arrivals," said O'Neill, smiling. "Actually, I had the computer alert me when your names appeared on the shuttle manifest. I confess that I didn't expect you back so soon."

Bakker shook his hand and said, "We had little choice in the matter. We ran into a few complications on Earth. It just seemed that we should come home."

"Complications?"

They walked toward the entrance. It was an open door that provided a good view of the Martian landscape beyond. A tabletop flatness that built into distant mountains of light red. The sky was light blue, never as deeply blue as the sky on Earth, and there were only a few wispy clouds that vanished almost as quickly as they formed. Off to the right was a short arc of a ridge line and a single, tall peak behind it marking an ancient impact crater.

"Yeah," said Hackett. "Apparently we aren't registered in their computers for something they called the social obligation list."

O'Neill wrinkled his brow and said, "Social obligation

list? Oh, you mean societal registration number. You don't have one?"

"No," said Hackett. "No such thing existed when we originally left Earth, and nothing like that was mentioned here on Mars. You should have known about it."

"Well, yes," said O'Neill, slightly embarrassed. "But we don't use those numbers on Mars, and I never thought about it. All that is too regimented for us. Too impersonal. I suppose as our population grows we'll have to come up with something similar, but right now we don't need it."

"But you have one of those numbers?" asked Bakker.

"Yes, but as I said, we simply don't use them. I have a disk with it on it, somewhere, as well as some other information. If I need it, I have it. I never thought about you two being outside the system."

"Someone should have thought of it, especially after some of our team returned to Earth," said Bakker.

O'Neill shrugged. He stopped and let the two of them exit first. He then waved a hand, and a cab slid up toward them. It ran on an electric motor and was hovering just above the ground on a cushion of air. It was one of the very rare private passenger vehicles on Mars.

As the door opened, O'Neill said, "Please enter."

"Why the royal treatment?" asked Hackett.

"Because I want you to meet some people in a little while."

Hackett looked at Bakker, who shrugged.

"Back to your other question," said O'Neill. "About this societal registration number. I never thought to check to see if you had one. It's issued at birth."

"Yeah, like the Social Security numbers that we do have," said Hackett.

The conversation dried up then. There was no point in going over it again. Everyone had the number, was issued the number at birth, and no one thought that neither Hackett nor Bakker would have one. It could be fixed easily. Now that they were back on Mars they could take care of it.

They entered the city, but Hackett wasn't interested in looking out the window. He knew what the city looked like. He had lived there when it was housed inside a dome, and he had lived there nearly two centuries later after terraforming had changed the landscape into something that humans could tolerate without the protection of a dome.

He was surprised when they left the city again and drove out onto what he thought of as a plain. Endless reddish sand that stretched to the horizon. Nothing spectacular about the scenery, and nothing that didn't exist on Earth in any of the great sand dune deserts scattered around the planet. The only difference was the color of the sand and the washed-out look of the cloudless sky above it.

It wasn't long before a building began to dominate the view and not much later that they stopped near that building. The doors opened, and O'Neill climbed out. When neither Hackett nor Bakker made a move to follow, he said, "Well, come on."

"I thought we were going home first. It's been a long and annoying trip," said Bakker. Her voice was tired and bordering on whiney.

"This won't take long," said O'Neill. He turned his attention to Hackett and added, "Besides, you're supposed to be in charge of the Galaxy Exploration Team. I thought you'd like to see what is being done."

"Well, yes, but exploration outside of the Solar System

has ended, so we don't really have a Galaxy Exploration Team anymore."

O'Neill gently directed them toward the doors of the largest building. He let them get ahead of him, and then hurried past them to open the small door in the larger hangar doors.

As he stepped through, Hackett surveyed the interior and asked, "What in the hell is this place?"

O'Neill smiled as the young men and women left the fish tank and began approaching them.

"This is your new team," said O'Neill, "and that," he added pointing at the fish tank, "is the means of travel."

Hackett stopped in his tracks. "We travel in that? How do you boost it into orbit?"

"We'll get to that," said O'Neill, "as soon as you meet your team."

Bakker leaned close and whispered, "I have a bad feeling about this."

Hackett laughed and said, "It can't be any worse than the last method they designed."

Bakker nodded, but she knew that it could be. Everything was always worse than it looked.

[4]

THEY MOVED TO THE FISH TANK AND ALL TOOK seats. A couple of extra chairs were brought in and pushed up against the table that had also been provided. They were sitting close to each other, which, on Mars, where people often went weeks without seeing another human in the flesh, made the enforced closeness nearly claustrophobic.

No one complained, but it was obvious that some of them were quite uncomfortable with the crowded conditions.

O'Neill, who hadn't taken a seat, actually took a step back from the group so that he was closer to the hatch. He smiled weakly and said, "Let's get started here. I think it would be helpful if we all introduced ourselves. And give us a little biographical note. We'll start with Bekka."

Cheney stood up and pushed her chair back away from the table, putting a little distance between her and the rest of the group. She hesitated, as if unsure about how to begin. Finally she told them who she was and how she happened to be involved in the project.

Her story was basically repeated by the others. All had been born on Mars, all had an interest in interplanetary travel and history but little real interest in interstellar flight and life on those far-flung planets. They all had trained in survival, observation, stealth, and a number of other strange skills that could be useful if they were tossed into planetary environments where no other human had ever been but that were similar to those found on Earth or Mars. They now understood the reason for some of the training, which had seemed so strange to them prior to their introduction to the fish tank. Cheney had mentioned the first, short hop to Earth and the others indicated that they had been on it, but added no real detail about it. A first experimental trip.

Hackett, of course, stunned the group by giving his birth date. The young people looked up in awe as they realized that his life had spanned more than two centuries. Things they read about, or viewed as history had been current events for him. The first of the faster-than-light missions had been the one that Hackett had made. They thought he might have known George Washington or that he had witnessed, in person, the first landings on the moon. It was as though they believed that anyone as old as Hackett must have been around for all distant historic events regardless of their dates.

They were even more surprised to learn that Bakker had discovered the first intelligent signal from outer space and had been on the team to verify it. She had launched, in a manner of speaking, the whole search for faster-than-light travel and had been the reason they were all now sitting there, on Mars, preparing to begin real galactic exploration.

To the young people, it was almost like being given the chance to meet Neil Armstrong or Magellan or Christopher Columbus. They could talk to a historical figure and ask the questions that no one had thought to ask two hundred years earlier.

O'Neill, however, didn't allow it right then. He wanted a team that could work together, not two separate teams, one of Hackett and Bakker, the oldsters, and the other made up of the youngsters. He was afraid that if he allowed the young people to question Hackett and Bakker for any period of time, they would all lose sight of the real goal. Galactic exploration.

And he had a tough time keeping the meeting in a language they all understood. The youngsters slipped into their verbal shorthand and the oldsters sometimes used archaic phrases and speech patterns that confounded everyone else.

O'Neill finally grew tired of the diversions, the bursts of verbal activity, and the questions that seemed so basic that everyone should already know the answers.

To move things along, he said, "Tomorrow we begin planning for a long-distance shoot. Several light-years from Earth. In the meantime, General Hackett and Doctor Bakker will be at home resting from their most recent journey. The rest of you, be able to function tomorrow at nine."

[5]

THE APARTMENT LOOKED JUST AS IT HAD WHEN they left it. The clothes that Bakker had thrown on the bed at the last minute were still there. The food in the pantry was still there and hadn't been attacked by insects or rodents, because there were no insects or rodents on Mars. People had learned from the examples on Earth, where transplanted rabbits overran parts of Australia and brown rats swarmed over the New World because there were no natural predators. As a result, isolation and new solutions were the order of the day on Mars.

There had been talk of introducing some of the insects that "cleaned" up after humans, but robots were considered cleaner and more efficient, and they didn't become pests.

Hackett walked into the front room, dropped his suitcase on the floor, and nearly fell onto the couch. He turned on the flat-screen and searched for the news, surprised to find that nothing had really changed. He had thought there would be major changes, until he remembered they hadn't actually been gone very long.

Bakker wandered through the apartment and then returned to the front room. She looked at Hackett and asked, "So now what?"

Hackett took a deep breath, muted the sound, and said, "I don't know."

"They're going to send us off into space."

"Well, it's not like we don't have the training."

"Which we got two hundred years ago."

Hackett nodded but said, "We haven't forgotten it, and survival in a hostile environment is still survival in a hostile environment."

"Except we don't know what all has been developed in the last two hundred years. I don't know a thing about surviving on an asteroid or a frozen moon until help arrives, but I'll bet there are people who do."

Hackett thought for a moment and said, "I don't think that's going to happen. We're only going into environments that mirror Earth's. The question is whether a rescue mission can be mounted if we get into trouble. That's the one thing I don't know."

Bakker turned and walked back into the bedroom for a moment but then returned. "I don't like this. There are too many questions I want to ask."

"I don't blame you, but, we're not required to do anything we don't want to do. I'm just wondering if they haven't given us this assignment so that we feel useful and not like a drain on society. Maybe that's the only reason we're involved here."

"Great. That makes me feel so much better." She left the room again.

Hackett turned up the sound and continued to watch the news. It was more like one of the old hometown weekly newspapers he remembered than a real news broadcast. The point of the broadcast was to provide a place where people could get their face on the news along with a little biographical information. It was more for ego boosts and maybe to stimulate a little societal interaction than to provide real news. News no longer consisted of important events of the day. It had devolved into a gossip column.

He watched with only half his mind. Instead he was thinking about what Bakker had said. They were being thrown into the mix with very little additional training. He didn't think it made a difference, given the nature of the trips, but there was always the unexpected. And that's what concerned him.

CHAPTER 8

[1]

THIS TIME THE MEETING WAS HELD IN A REAL conference room, one that had been designed with the personal-space considerations of Martians figured in. It might have been the enforced crowding on the ships that brought them from Earth or it might have been a result of the limited space available before the terraforming, but whatever the reason, Martians took up more personal space than humans did.

The conference began with a round of briefings, which was followed by a video of the target world that had been sent back by the unoccupied fish tank. Then there had been discussions about survival techniques for the team sent, should that become necessary. There had even been additional training, based on the almost constant rain that fell on the target world.

For hours, Hackett and Bakker studied the video that had been supplied by the robot probe, looking for anything that might be either dangerous or helpful. They were looking into a world where the jungle was dense and the vegetation looked remarkably Earth-like. Tall trees with broad leaves, few bushes, and no flowering plants that they could see. There were lots of what might be called ferns. They could see no visible grasses and no fruit-bearing trees. It gave them the feel of a primitive world where the plants and trees were just beginning to diversify.

O'Neill, who, as he always did, stood at the head of the table and directed the discussion, said, "Little evidence of animal life and few insects. Nothing very large or dangerous."

Bakker asked, "How far away is the target world?"

"Based on our calculations, based on the power consumption, I would say that it's something on the order of eight to ten light-years distant."

"Then you don't know where it is?"

O'Neill looked embarrassed. He didn't have a good answer, and he didn't understand the physics of determining the distance. He thought of it as magic, beyond his comprehension. He said, "Not exactly. But that's just me. The project directors believe that it is out beyond Alpha Centauri a ways. Remember, these are our best guesses based on the catalog that we've built over the last several days."

He grinned and said, "And that is part of the mission. To get photographs of the night sky so that we can determine, based on the star positions, exactly where you went. As the missions continue, we'll be able to build a catalog of destinations and distances. We can begin to finely calibrate the equipment so we don't have to do best-guess."

Hackett laughed. "I love doing this. We don't know where you're going, we don't really know how long it will take, but it doesn't look dangerous, at least to those remaining behind."

"The probe made it without difficulty. The atmosphere is near Earth normal, though the proportion of gasses is slightly different. Nothing that would be fatal. The fish tank is made of bulletproof acrylic. It can withstand a substantial shock, so you have a safe haven. You can initiate the return at any time, but you are scheduled for fifty-two hours on the planet. There is nothing for you to worry about."

"Yeah, that's what they said about faster-than-life, but no one figured on the time dilation increase either. There is something that can always go wrong," said Bakker. "Murphy's Law demands it."

Hackett grinned and added, "And that's what they told the passengers on the *Titanic*. It was only a little bump. There is nothing for you to worry about. Go back to sleep, and we'll be under way shortly."

"Who is Murphy?" asked O'Neill.

Hackett laughed out loud but said, "A prophet in the ancient world who said that if anything can go wrong, it will go wrong. It's a principle to live by."

Clark, who had remained silent, spoke up, "Hey, we've done this before and it works. You want to stay behind old-timer, then you can. I'm ready to explore our universe."

Hackett turned slowly to look at Clark, who had a smug look on his face, almost as if he believed he was the brightest person on Mars. And the bravest.

Hackett said, "I can still take you, smart-ass."

Bakker barked a laugh. "If you two children are finished beating your chests . . . ?"

Now Hackett laughed. "Of course. I shouldn't let the punk get under my skin."

"Gentlemen," said O'Neill, "save your energy for the voyage. Now, if I may continue?"

Hackett shrugged, and Clark nodded.

For the next hour they studied the video, listened to the recorded sounds that included a thunderstorm in what might have been the middle of the afternoon. They weren't sure of the time of day, because the planet's sun was not visible through the jungle's thick canopy. Shafts of sunlight cut through, and their angle suggested it was afternoon. It seemed the sun was lowering, but they didn't know the planet's rotational cycle. The robot and the fish tank had remained on the surface for only a couple of hours.

O'Neill finally wound down and asked, "Are there any questions?"

"Why fifty-two hours?" asked Hackett. "Forty-eight I can understand. Even sixty, but fifty-two seems arbitrary."

"I suppose it is somewhat, but that puts you back here in the middle of the morning and gives us most of the day for debriefings. With the scheduled rest periods, it shouldn't be a strain on any of you, although the last day might be a bit long."

"All of us are going?"

"No," said O'Neill. "I'm sorry. I should have covered that. We'll keep four people here as backup. Hackett will go, and Bakker will stay here."

Hackett looked at O'Neill. "Once again that seems a bit arbitrary. Besides, Bakker as an astronomer would be better equipped to determine the position of the planet than me. She has a better feel for what is in the night sky."

"I don't think I would be able to figure out anything using just a visual reference," said Bakker. "I'd need computer access, and you can send anything that I need back to me."

Hackett shrugged. "I stand corrected."

O'Neill put both hands on the table as if to stand but remained seated. He said, "If no one has any additional questions or comments, then we need to get ready. Launch is in two hours and forty minutes."

[2]

HACKETT HAD EXPECTED SOME SORT OF ADDI-tional briefing, some sort of additional instruction, but that wasn't what happened. Instead he, along with the other travelers—Clark, Langston, Cheney, and Novotny—went to lunch. Nothing heavy, nothing exciting, just a nutritious meal that provided for high energy, in case it was needed later. A relaxing meal served before they were sent off into the unknown, and possible death at the hands, or tentacles or teeth, of some strange alien beast that recognized them as little more than dinner.

They then were herded into a locker room to change into traveling clothes. The uniforms were rip resistant and had long sleeves and long pants, with Velcro around the wrists and ankles so that they could be fastened tightly. They were also given boots, gloves, goggles, and a face mask. They were given little in the way of equipment to carry, most of that was already stored in the fish tank, along with a variety of weapons.

Hackett thought about that and didn't like it. As a military man, he recognized the importance of being familiar with a weapon before needing to use it. Civilians seemed to think that you just picked up a rifle, aimed, fired, and the bullet struck home. They knew nothing of zeroing a weapon for the peculiarities of the specific marksman, that it was important to be familiar with all the weapon's vagaries. Martians, having never been forced into violent confrontation with their fellows, didn't think about those things.

Now fed and clothed, they walked back to the center of the hangar and to the fish tank. The equipment someone figured they would need was inside, including food and water, survey gear, and the weapons.

Hackett stopped short, looked through the glass and then back at the corner of the hangar, where the control room was situated. He could see figures moving around behind the protective glass, but he didn't recognize any of them.

Clark stepped up to the hatch and opened it. He looked back at Hackett. "You coming, or what?"

Hackett wondered where Bakker was. He'd expected her to be there, but then, the voyage wasn't going to be far. He'd be gone a little over two days. Hardly much of a trip. He had to get that into his mind. It wasn't much of a trip. Probably no more dangerous than any journey on Mars and probably safer than getting into a ship to travel around the Solar System. Surely safer than riding in a car on a freeway on Earth had been two hundred years ago. Certainly safer than getting into a wagon to cross the expanse of the American frontier three hundred years ago.

Hackett walked to the fish tank and climbed through the hatch. He joined the others, sitting down, while Clark closed the hatch behind him. When Clark finished, he sat down, too.

"How long does this take?" asked Hackett.

He noticed that his voice had taken on a strange quality, reverberating inside the fish tank. The people and his surroundings took on an unreal quality—blurred, with double and triple ghostly images. Motion seemed to stop and repeat itself, almost like a film that was doubled back on itself, except that it moved forward at an unnatural pace.

The answer to his question, seeming to come from the bottom of a distant well was, "Not too long. Time sort of stops for the trip."

And then, almost immediately, the world outside the fish tank shifted slightly, once, twice, and then coalesced into the vivid colors of a new world. Trees, bushes, ferns, and other plants appeared all around them. Deep greens and browns, with light shafts breaking through the canopy.

Clark was on his feet immediately, shaking off the effects of the trip. He said, "Let's take a look around the fish tank. Make sure that our site is secure."

"That's it?" asked Hackett, surprised.

"I don't know what you expected, but that's it. We have a set procedure to follow."

"Where are we?"

Cheney moved toward the water and picked up a bottle. "We don't know yet. That's why we have to make a survey of the sky tonight."

"Which means," said Clark, "we have to leave the fish tank to travel. I don't see much of the sky here."

"Let's hope for a clearing close to us," said Novotny. "I'm not in the mood for a long walk."

Hackett moved toward one of the glass walls and almost put his nose against it, like a little kid outside a toy store wanting to see everything inside.

But there wasn't much to see. Only plant life, with no visible sign of animal life. He could see nothing moving, but then the sudden appearance of the fish tank might have frightened any animals in the area.

Clark had the hatch opened and had stepped back. Cheney, with her water in hand, began to move toward the hatch. Then, Clark, apparently realizing that no human had ever set foot on the planet, stepped in front of her and stepped through the hatch before she could get out.

He grinned and said, "I declare this planet will be known as Clark's World."

Novotny laughed, and Hackett said, "Shouldn't we vote on a name?"

"Why? We can call the next one we get to Hackett's World if you want."

"We have no rules for naming the planets," said Langston. "We can call them whatever we want, and I suspect, in a few months, we're going to run out of names."

Hackett looked at her, figuring she was probably right.

[3]

BAKKER HADN'T BEEN READY FOR THE FISH tank to simply disappear. It popped out of existence like someone had thrown a switch on a light. One instant it was there, in the center of the hangar, and the next it was gone, leaving only a few marks on the polished surface of the hangar floor.

"Successful launch," said one of the technicians, unnecessarily.

"How long does the trip take?" asked Bakker.

O'Neill, who was watching one of the monitors, said, "It's nearly instantaneous. I think those traveling are aware of some passage of time in the fish tank, but it's only moments. Hardly long enough to take a deep breath."

Bakker turned and looked at one of the flat-screens mounted on the wall. She could see the interior of the fish tank and see the people moving around inside it, though she couldn't hear what they were saying.

"Don't we have sound?"

Another of the technicians touched a button to her right, and Bakker heard Hackett say, "Give me one of those water bottles, please."

On another of the screens Bakker looked out on the alien world. It looked almost like Earth, though the plants had a more primitive look to them. It was the large ferns that gave her that impression. She always thought of ferns belonging to the Triassic, though there were modern ferns all over Earth and more than a few that had been transplanted to Mars. Still that was how she had been conditioned to think by a hundred movies about lost worlds and a thousand paintings of what Earth had looked like in the age of the dinosaurs.

"What do we do now?" asked Bakker.

"Monitor the activity. Record everything we can for analysis later. Look for trouble that our team might not have seen and warn them about that. Just relax here and watch, listen, and learn."

Bakker found a chair and sat down. She realized that she was watching the exploration of a new world. She was seeing it in nearly real time and was almost as much of a participant as those who had gone off in the fish tank. The only difference was that the danger was real to them. She was as safe as she would have been in her apartment watching a documentary.

CHAPTER 9

[1]

WHEN IT BECAME CLEAR TO O'NEILL THAT THE mission was moving along smoothly, he slipped from the control room in the corner of the hangar and left the building. He took a magnetic bus into the city and walked along the grass-covered sidewalks until he reached the administration building. He was not greeted by either a guard or a receptionist. There was no need for either on Mars.

O'Neill took the elevator up two floors, exited into a long, brightly lit hallway, walked nearly to the end, and entered what he thought of as a lecture hall.

The room had a steeply slanted floor with rows of seats rising up fifteen or twenty feet. Opposite the seats was something like an orchestra pit that held a conference table, and beyond that was a slightly raised stage, where a lecturer might stand. Most of the time the "lecturer" was a holographic image that materialized either above the stage or centered on the conference table.

As O'Neill entered, he found Sally Clinton, Bryon Davis, and William Curry already waiting. Above the conference table was a small picture that was being transmitted from the fish tank. They didn't notice him as he entered, their attention focused on the slowly rotating image above them.

"I see that the hookup is working well," he said to announce himself.

Without looking, Clinton said, "And you expected anything else?"

He pulled a chair out and sat down. "No. Anything of interest happening?"

"They're still inside the fish tank, but they've taken some measurements, and they've discussed their exploration mission this evening. None of them seems too keen about leaving the fish tank now, though Clark stepped out quickly and claimed the privilege of naming the world."

"Should I guess at the name he chose?"

Clinton laughed. "He's the one with the ego. He named it after himself."

"He has an ego, all right," said O'Neill, chuckling. "I thought we had bred that out of the population some time ago."

"Langston made the point that we'd be exploring lots of worlds. Everyone will have a chance to name a world after themselves," said Clinton.

"Yes, but the first world we conquer with this system will be named for Clark. A little immortality for him that none of us thought about," O'Neill said.

Clinton waved a hand, now bored with the conversation. "It doesn't matter."

O'Neill studied the image for a moment. Finally he said, "I don't think I blame them for hesitating. I'm not sure I'd want to leap into a new world."

Davis looked over at O'Neill and asked, "Is this going to work?"

"Obviously," said O'Neill. "We're looking at the fish tank sitting on another planet."

"That's not what I mean," said Davis.

"This is not the place to discuss that," warned Curry. "This is not a secure location."

O'Neill ignored the warning. He said, "Of course it's going to work. Isn't that obvious?"

Clinton said, "Yes, it'll work, but I have to tell you, this is becoming boring."

Now O'Neill laughed. "Ah, the younger generation. Has to be entertained every waking second and then wants dreams transmitted into their brains like long-lost television shows, so they won't be bored while they sleep and won't have to expend the energy to make up the dreams."

"It's not that," said Clinton failing to rise to the bait. "They're not doing anything."

[2]

THERE SEEMED TO BE NOTHING DANGEROUS outside the fish tank. Environmental conditions were close to Earth normal. They could protect themselves from predators, though no one expected predators to be a problem.

"Most predators attack a rather small variety of prey

and rarely change their habits unless they're forced to do so," said Novotny, sounding like he was trying to convince himself. "Besides, predators on this world probably wouldn't recognize humans as prey and probably wouldn't find us edible anyway."

Hackett grinned at that and said, "Then we'll have to hope that they're not territorial."

Clark shrugged. "I've seen nothing that is large enough, or agile enough to take us on out there, and there is nothing on the sensors to suggest that something like that is hiding. Let's go exploring."

Hackett went to the case where the weapons were stored, took one for himself, and handed one to each of the others. "It doesn't hurt to be prepared, just in case."

They opened the hatch, exited, and then stood for a moment, outside in the New World. As they started to move away from the fish tank, Hackett asked, "Are we going to leave anyone behind as a rear guard?"

That stopped Clark. "I hadn't thought about that, and it never came up in training. We just assumed that the fish tank would be sealed behind us and nothing would be able to violate its integrity."

"Look," said Novotny, "I'll stay behind. I don't really want to go for a long walk. Sound's like too much work."

Hackett looked back at him, curious. "I thought you all had adventurous natures."

"Sometimes my feet hurt," said Novotny.

"I'll stay, too," said Langston. "Sort of a backup."

"If we're ready," said Clark. "Let's get this show on the road."

They started off, found a break in the trees and what looked like an animal trail. Hackett knew the disadvantages of following such a trail, but there were no enemy soldiers concealed in the bush and no reason to suspect an ambush from intelligent creatures. Predators were another matter, but he was sure their weapons could eliminate any such threat if the predator didn't flee from them immediately.

They moved slowly, spread out but staying close enough so that they could see and protect one another. They tried not to touch anything, not knowing what might be toxic. Plants on Earth defended themselves with a variety of irritants, some of which could be fatal if not treated properly. Who knew what might be growing on this new world?

They came to a stream that was as clear as glass. The stones in the bottom had been rounded and polished by the action of the water. Hackett hesitated there, searching for fish, but saw nothing. He hoped to see, at the very least, some kind of insect, but there was nothing living in or around the stream. That worried him, though he wasn't sure why.

They crossed the stream, moved deeper into the trees, and suddenly popped out into a clearing. There was a slight rise toward the grass-covered center, making it look as if there was a hump in the middle. It was ringed with trees and bushes, but as they stepped out, they could see a nearly clear blue sky with a single, puffy cloud drifting by.

Before they walked out into the sunshine, they flipped down the filters on their goggles. They were all used to the reduced sunlight on Mars. None of them except Hackett had ever lived on a world with a bright ball of light in the sky, and he hadn't lived on Earth in years. Their eyes would be sensitive to the bright light.

Hackett held up a hand to shadow his eyes and looked up toward the sun. He said, "Looks just like the sun from Earth. Big and bright."

"Too bright," said Cheney. "I don't like it."

"Sure reminds me of Earth," said Hackett.

"What'd you expect?" asked Clark. "We're selecting only Earth normal planets."

"I don't know," said Hackett. "Something a little different from Earth."

"You should see some of the worlds we saw on the trial tapes. Barren rocks with constant storms. Worlds that are awash with water and little land. Worlds with atmospheres that are nearly poisonous to us, or worlds so hot that metal would melt and run in rivers. Others so cold that nothing lives while blizzards swirl endlessly. We had to cast about looking for anything that is even close to suitable," said Cheney.

"Well, this strikes me as quite Earth-like, though the plants don't look much like the trees or bushes on Earth. Maybe precursors to them or something."

Clark knelt and shed his pack. He dug through it but then simply let it lie. He looked around, studying the scenery without saying a word.

"I would expect animal life," said Hackett.

"Why not a world with only plants?" asked Cheney.

"These are highly adapted plants," said Hackett. "It suggests a long period of evolution, and I would expect something more mobile to have evolved, in that time."

"So we just haven't seen it yet," said Clark.

"I suppose," said Hackett slowly. "I suppose everything

could be running away from us. But I would have thought
we would have heard something."

"Are you worried?" asked Clark.

"No, just surprised," said Hackett.

He then sat down and pulled his pack from his back. He
leaned back, looking up into the sky. The cloud was gone,
leaving them with nothing to see except the bright blue and
a tiny crescent of a natural satellite.

"Just like Earth," said Hackett.

"Not just like Earth," corrected Clark, "but damned
close. Very damned close."

[3]

NIGHT CAME AS IT DID ON EARTH, WITH THE
sunlight fading gradually. They couldn't see the sun because of the trees, but they assumed that it set as it did on
Earth and Mars. It was now dark, and Hackett waited for
the jungle around him to come alive with animals running
around and calling to one another or searching for one another, but it didn't. No sudden cries of animals on the hunt
or on the make. No swarms of insects looking for something to eat or something to annoy. No rustling of leaves
and bushes of larger animals searching for one another to
mate or to eat. It was as quiet as anything he had ever
heard, the only sounds came from his companions, and the
only light from the artificial illumination they had brought
with them.

The night was cloudless. The sky was bright with stars,
but Hackett saw none of the constellations that he knew.

He was still in the same galaxy. He'd expected to see a hint of the Milky Way.

Langston was sitting in the tall, dry grass, looking up at the stars. She glanced over to Hackett and said, "I don't see anything familiar."

"Neither do I," said Hackett, "but, even if we traveled only a relatively short distance, there might not be anything for us to recognize."

Clark had set up the camera on the tripod and had pointed it up toward the sky. He stepped away from it and pushed the button. There was a whirring as the camera began to work, the noise an artificial creation to tell the photographer that pictures were being taken. The tiny motor on the tripod turned the camera so that a panorama of the sky was taken. The pictures could be of value in identifying the planet's location.

"When this is finished," said Hackett, "there is really no reason for us to remain here."

"No," said Clark. "But I don't want to go stumbling around in the dark. If we get lost, we could be truly screwed. Besides there is also no reason not to stay in place overnight. Give a look at the sky in a couple of hours."

Hackett sat down and leaned back. He laced his fingers behind his head and looked up, directly overhead. The stars were quite bright, several of them seeming to be first magnitude or brighter. He searched for something he recognized, but the organization of the stars looked as if someone had splattered white paint on a charcoal background. He saw no familiar patterns.

After a while he began to see some patterns, but they were not those he knew from home. There was no Orion or

Orion's Belt, no Canis Major or Ursa Major, though he did see something that resembled the Big Dipper. It was somewhat misshapen, as if it had been well used and then banged on the ground or maybe stepped on or run over. It wasn't really *the* Big Dipper.

The camera continued to take pictures, mapping the whole sky above them. Finally, it shifted around, taking the last of the photos of the zenith. It stopped then, falling quiet.

"We done now?" asked Hackett, still looking upward.

"For the moment. You have somewhere you have to be soon?" asked Clark.

"Nope."

"Then just relax."

"I wish I could, but I feel like something is about to fall on us."

"What would that be?"

"I haven't the faintest idea."

[4]

NATURALLY, THERE WAS TRANSMISSION BE-tween the camera in the clearing and the fish tank sitting about a mile away. Naturally, there was transmission between the fish tank on the new world and the home base, which might have been light-years away, but with the "window" or "gate" open, they could communicate with the same ease as two people on telephones. That meant that the pictures taken by Clark's camera in the clearing were being sent back to the team who was on Mars. Those people, including Bakker, were seeing the pictures almost as they were being taken.

Bakker sat in a small domed room off the control room, stuck in the corner of the hangar, and watched as each photograph was displayed on the big flat-screen. The detail was extraordinary, and by touching a button, she could create a holographic display that would allow her to step into the picture. It would seem to her as if she was standing on the planet and looking up into its night sky.

She could, if she wanted, allow the scene to change as each photograph was transmitted, or she could freeze it until she was ready for the next picture. And once all the pictures were taken, she could slowly rotate the images so that it seemed as if she was spinning on the planet, watching the night sky.

O'Neill had returned from his meeting and was sitting next to her, making no comment. He seemed to be fairly blasé about everything, as if he had done this a hundred times before.

Finally, as they returned to the first of the pictures, Bakker said, "I don't see anything familiar."

"Did you expect to?"

"Depends on the distance. Depends on the direction. I would expect to recognize something, unless we've gone much farther than we thought."

"But to recognize something with the unaided eye?"

Bakker shrugged. "Well, that was a long shot, but I think once we begin analysis, we should see something."

She stood up, walked to the screen, and reached out to touch it, as if it had texture that would tell her something about what she was seeing. She scanned the picture slowly but still could find nothing she recognized.

"After computer analysis, we should have something," she said almost as if trying to convince herself.

O'Neill sat quietly, watching the scene change from one star field to the next. Had the pictures been of the sky seen from Mars, he probably wouldn't have recognized anything. Astronomy was not one of the sciences he followed. It was too involved with math and observations of celestial objects far away. He liked something a little closer to home.

Bakker let the pictures rotate through their sequences without stopping them. After an hour or so, a new set of pictures began to appear, but the star fields remained unfamiliar.

The sliver of a moon appeared in the last of the pictures. It looked like a glowing fingernail thrown into the sky and was reminiscent of Earth's moon in its earliest or latest phase. There was no detail available, so Bakker couldn't tell if it was as pockmarked as Earth's moon, though she thought she could see hints of craters.

Finally, she leaned back in her chair, stretched her arms high over her head, and announced, "I'm tired. I'm really very tired."

"No reason for you to remain here," said O'Neill.

"I hate leaving the area in case something interesting happens."

"We have arranged sleep accommodations for those who wish to remain on-site," he said.

"Then I'll grab some sleep. I think, after I rest, I'll run some simulations and some other tests and see if I can identify anything in the star field."

"What kind of luck do you think you'll have?" asked O'Neill as he stood.

"Not much without more data. I can look at everything we've gathered and then think of some questions that I should ask and see if the people in the field can get answers for me."

"Can you identify the sky from that planet?"

"If it's not too far away from us."

But she had no idea how far it was.

CHAPTER 10

[1]

DAWN CAME WITHOUT THE CACOPHONY THAT greeted the dawn on Earth. There was a gentle rustling of the leaves, as a light breeze blew through the treetops, but no cries from birds or animals and no buzz of insects. The jungle was as green as any on Earth, but there was no sign of animal life.

Overhead were a few light, puffy clouds that quickly burned off as the sun rose. Around them were lower hanging clouds, fog really, dense and white, obscuring some of the jungle and giving the impression that something had caught fire.

Hackett stood up, having slept poorly, because he'd slept on the ground. He hadn't worried about anything creeping up on him, because they'd found no evidence that anything like that existed. But the ground was damp and the night had been a little cool.

Of course, he hadn't planned on sleeping, but after the first set of photographs had been taken and transmitted back to the fish tank, there wasn't much else to do. No one wanted to risk exploration in the dark, because no one wanted to get lost on a new world. They had methods to track one another and there was a rally beacon on the fish tank, but electronic gadgets sometimes failed, and sometimes they failed in sequence, causing a spectacular screwup.

But it was a moot point, because the tracking devices still worked and Hackett knew how to find the fish tank. Their trail through the jungle had been well marked for them, but Hackett couldn't figure out what had marked it. Trails required feet and movement, and there seemed to be nothing here with feet to have created the trail, and there certainly wasn't anything that moved along it.

Clark was holding a digital camera and focusing on a tree across the clearing. Its base was enclosed in fog, but the top was glowing brightly in the morning sun. It was an impressive sight, and Clark took several pictures of it.

"That'll make a stunning photo," said Hackett.

"I thought so, too," said Clark.

He finished with that and began a slow turn, searching the jungle for something else to photograph.

"Today's schedule?" asked Hackett.

"I thought we would return to the fish tank, slowly, examining everything between here and there. Then, sunlight permitting, take off in another direction to explore a little more of this world."

"Looking for animal life?"

"Yeah. I just can't see a situation where you could develop plant life of such complexity but not have some sort of animal evolve as well."

"Seems to me that there were islands in the Pacific a thousand years ago like that."

"Nope," said Clark. "Not ones with only robust plant life. Some sort of animal life always managed to get there and certainly lots of birds."

"Well, it's not an area of my expertise," said Hackett.

Cheney woke up, stood up, and stretched. She grinned broadly and said, "This certainly wasn't as much fun as I thought it was going to be."

"I would like to make a serious search for some kind of animal life," said Clark.

"Then have us spread out around the clearing, keeping it as the rally point, and let's see what we can find," said Hackett.

"After breakfast?" asked Cheney.

"You can eat breakfast as you move," said Clark.

"Is there any reason for haste?" asked Hackett. "Is there something else that you want to know?"

Clark took another picture and then lowered the camera. "We have a tight time frame on this world."

"Yes," agreed Hackett, "but taking a few minutes to eat isn't going to upset the schedule."

"Fine," said Clark less than reasonably. "Eat. Hell, cook a huge breakfast over a roaring campfire and then sit back to let it digest."

Hackett looked at him for a moment and then decided it was time for a lesson in courtesy. "I don't think we should make a fire, because we don't know what will burn and what won't, and we certainly don't want to start a fire that would burn up half the jungle by accident. We don't need to take time gathering wood, and we certainly don't want to go chopping down trees when we don't have to. It is not a requirement that we have a warm breakfast. We could eat it cold, saving a few minutes. But, there are heating tabs on the rations, which will cook the meals quickly. In the end, there is no reason to be rude."

Clark gave him an angry glare, but said nothing. He walked away, putting the camera in his pocket. He stopped at the edge of the jungle but didn't enter it.

"This isn't a bad world," said Cheney trying to change the subject.

"No," said Hackett. "It's not a bad world, but it's a little too deserted to suit me. I'd like to find some kind of animal life."

[2]

SARAH BAKKER'S EYES BURNED FROM LACK OF sleep. Though she tried to rest, she had been excited by the pictures transmitted through the fish tank. She had hoped to figure out the star fields so that she would be able to plot the location of the world they had found and learn how far they had traveled, but the task was taking much longer than she expected. Nothing looked familiar, and unless the new world was thousands of light-years from Earth, she believed she would find something.

Now, with dawn breaking on Mars, as it had on the new world, she found that she was tired. The star fields had yielded nothing of importance. She had identified types of stars, and she had identified what she believed to be a planet in the star field. There was even a faint streak that might have been a meteor, but there was nothing recognizable as constellations and certainly nothing that provided her with a clue as to location.

Finally, she rocked back in the chair, rubbed her eyes, and looked around. The two technicians who had been assisting her, one male and one female, had fallen asleep. Both were young, but both were less than enthusiastic about figuring out where the new world was located in relation to Mars or the rest of the Solar System.

Without waking them, Bakker stood up and found herself a warm cup of coffee. She drank it without sugar or cream, hoping that the caffeine would make her feel better, or at least wake her up.

Sipping the coffee, she stood staring at one screen that showed a portion of the star field and at another that was flashing through a series of star fields, attempting to find a pattern that would match, in part, the patterns seen from Earth. She was glad that she didn't have to attempt to make the recognition manually. She wouldn't have been able to do so.

After a moment, she said, out loud, though quietly, "I wonder if progression makes any difference?"

Jenny, the younger of the two technicians, stirred, opened her eyes, and asked sleepily, "Did you say something?"

Jenny was an undergraduate who had a real interest in astronomy. Her passion for the work overcame her rather pedestrian intellect. She worked harder to understand the nuances of the science.

Bakker looked at her and started to say something, but stopped. She cocked her head to the side as if listening, and said, "I was thinking that we're looking for a pattern in a star field that probably is different than we think. I mean, we haven't adjusted for a time difference. The light from the stars we see here on Mars is the light that left the star years ago. And everything is in motion in the galaxy. So we need to adjust for that."

Now the male technician, Jim, sat up. He looked bleary eyed and only half awake. His dark hair was mussed, and his beard had grown out. He was one of those males who refused to use a depilatory because he enjoyed the daily shaving ritual. It made him feel better. Now it just made him look scruffy and a little irresponsible.

"I thought the computer compensated for that."

"Yes," said Bakker, "but we compensated for it from a position here on Mars. Maybe we need to think in terms of a progression from the point of view of the star system where the photographs were taken."

"That's impossible," said Jenny. "We don't know exactly where that system is."

"Difficult, yes," said Bakker, "but we have the computer capability for it. It's really just a question of setting the right parameters and searching for patterns."

"We don't know how far the new world is, or in what direction, or anything else."

"That will make our success all that more impressive," said Bakker. "Besides, we do have some indications about where the fish tank went, and we can use that to establish the baseline. This is possible."

Jim looked at her and said, "Is there anything that ever gets you down?"

"Why would it?" asked Bakker. She smiled as she said

it, thinking that it had been a strange thing to say at that particular moment.

She turned her attention back to the screens. She still saw nothing that matched the pictures sent back. As she watched the parade of data, she knew that the task was much more difficult than she had let on. She had believed that a trip of a short distance would change the star fields, but change would be small and there would be something in them that either she or the computer would recognize.

But there was nothing. It told her that the trip might have been farther than anticipated and that their calculations had, therefore, been off. She wasn't immediately sure how to correct for that, other than to try to compensate for the motion of the stars, projecting the time line backward for the present. That might provide a glimpse of star fields that she recognized.

For success, she only needed to find one tiny pattern in the star fields. She just needed that single, small clue. But it didn't look as if she was going to find that.

To the technicians, she said, "What we do is have the computer change the perspective, looking at the stars as they would appear from Sirius or Tau Ceti. Such a search would eat up a great deal of computer time and could take days or weeks to accomplish, but it could be done."

"What you're saying," said Jim, "is that we need only to write the program to make the search and allow it to run while we do something else."

"Well, yes."

"Then it's not a real problem for us, but one for the computer."

"We need to design the specific parameters, but yes, really, it becomes a computer problem. And, I think we have to compensate for time. With that, we should have some success."

[3]

THE WALK BACK TO THE FISH TANK, THROUGH the pristine jungle, again crossing the clear stream that looked artificial, was uneventful. They still found no trace of animal life, found no insects, and found nothing wiggling on the ground. Just the jungle filled with plants and trees and even flowers.

Hackett stopped to examine one of the flowers and identified the various components half-remembered from high school biology: petals, stamen, and pestle. He wondered how the flowers were pollinated. There were so many relationships among the plants and animals and insects on Earth, which spread pollen. Here, without the animals or insects, there was obviously a mechanism for pollinating that Hackett couldn't see.

They arrived back at the fish tank. Novotny was sitting in one of the chairs like a man lounging in his living room watching television. He looked like he was half asleep, maybe slightly bored. When he spotted the rest of the team coming in, he barely moved.

Clark opened the hatch, and the team entered the fish tank. Novotny stood up and asked, "Anything interesting?"

"Nope," said Clark. "Just more jungle. Did get the star fields for Bakker, but nothing else."

Hackett dropped into the closest chair, surprised at how drained he felt. It hadn't seemed that hot or humid, and the trip hadn't been very far. The only thing he could attribute his tiredness to was that he hadn't slept well the night before.

Cheney, looking fresh and rested, grinned and said, "We found a nice stream if we need to bathe."

"We have about twenty-four hours left," said Clark. "There are a number of things we could do in that time. Explore around the fish tank, maybe move out in a different direction and see what we can find."

"But you don't think so," said Hackett.

"If we had seen anything suggesting animal life, I would be inclined to explore further, but all we've seen are the plants and trees."

"We need to gather some biological samples of those," said Hackett.

"Something we can do in the next hour right around here," said Clark.

"Yes," said Hackett, "but . . ." He trailed off. He was going to suggest they range a little farther out, but he knew that they would have seen something already if there were animals to be found. They were on a virtual island populated only by plant life.

Novotny said, "I want to get out of here for a while. I'll get some of the plant samples."

"Let's not take more than an hour or so for that," said Clark.

"Why?"

"Because I said so."

Hackett laughed. "I think you'll need a better reason than that. We've got the time, and there is no reason to not make a complete survey."

"Fine," said Clark. "Knock yourselves out."

Novotny picked up the collection kit and moved to the hatch. He stopped there and said, "Anyone else interested?"

"Sure," said Langston. "I'm tired of looking at the same thing."

"I'll go, too," said Hackett, "but I'll go in a different direction."

Cheney said, "And I'll go, too. I'll get some of the water in the steam and maybe walk along it for a while. See what I can find upstream."

They all left the fish tank together. Novotny and Langston took off in one direction, Hackett in another, and Cheney back toward the stream. None of them found anything of great interest.

Cheney had hoped to find something living in the stream, but could find nothing to suggest any animal life anywhere. She gathered her samples and headed back to the fish tank. When she got there, she found the rest of the team.

"So," said Clark, "now we wait."

Hackett sat down, staring out of the fish tank at the jungle around them, and couldn't think of anything else they needed to do. They had the samples, and they had the photographs of the star fields. They had accomplished everything they needed to do. In the morning, when they were recalled, they would have briefings. It could turn into a long day.

Clark said, "I think we need to take it easy now. If you all are through running around in the jungle."

"I'm ready for recall," said Hackett.

CHAPTER 11

[1]

HACKETT HAD EXPECTED A FULL-BLOWN DE-
briefing when they returned from the new world, but that
didn't happen. And, as he thought about it, he wondered
about isolation to determine if they had been exposed to
any alien microorganisms that could infect the human population of Mars. No one had discussed that with him and
he hadn't thought, earlier, to ask the specific question. He
was surprised by the cavalier attitude toward dropping humans into an unknown environment and then plucking
them out again without a thought about the possibilities of
some kind of foreign contamination.

But, when the fish tank was recalled and reappeared in
the hangar on Mars, it was too late to protect against anything deadly that might have attached itself to the fish tank
on this trip. If there was anything, there was a possibility

that they might be able to isolate it in the hangar or one small section of Mars, but no one seemed to think about it. The moment the fish tank arrived, the crew exited. Within minutes they were all on the way to a preliminary debriefing.

That preliminary briefing was held in a conference room in one of the buildings near the hangar. It was a long, low structure with a single visible door and no windows that Hackett could see. The roof looked flat, and the building itself looked like some kind of machine shed from a farm of the late twentieth century back on Earth.

The conference room didn't look any more ornate than the outside of the building. Just a table surrounded by a few chairs, a concrete floor or a reasonable facsimile of concrete, and a single, large, dominant light overhead. Hackett was sure there was a method of projecting images into the room, but he couldn't spot the holo.

Hackett pulled out a chair, dropped into it, and then stared at the others as they entered and sat down around the table. The whole team, including those who hadn't gone on the trip, trooped in singly or in pairs. They were arrayed around the table with O'Neill, as usual, standing at the head.

Without preamble, O'Neill said, "Did anyone see anything of note that wasn't already communicated to us during the journey?"

Hackett waited until the others had answered the question and then said, "I'm worried about contamination."

"Meaning?"

"Microbes."

"I've had that discussion, with the others," said O'Neill. He waved a hand as if dismissing the question.

"Well, I missed it."

O'Neill looked at the other travelers and saw that none of them really cared if he went over it again. In fact, it didn't look as if any of them were even listening to the discussion.

O'Neill sat down and said, somewhat exasperated, "It was something that concerned everyone from the beginning of space flight going back to the old Apollo program in the mid-twentieth century."

"Yes, yes," interrupted Hackett. "I know all that. We found nothing on the moon or on Mars that could infect us as we moved off Earth. No biological life at all on the moon or on Mars, though there were hints that life had once started on Mars."

"And the few extraterrestrial microbes we did find," said O'Neill, "on Io and on Triton, were so different from Earth-based-life that there was no possibility of cross-contamination. These microorganisms could not infect us, and if they were transported into our environment, even the most benign of environments, from our point of view, they died. Conditions here were too harsh for them from their perspective."

"You expect those observations to hold up across all the worlds we plan to visit?"

"General Hackett," said O'Neill in a tired voice, "we have a long history of study in this arena, and we have implemented the necessary precautions based on the best evidence we have. If you study the history of disease on Earth, you'll realize that there are many diseases that do not cross species lines. There are very few diseases that can, for example, infect both reptiles and mammals. There are many diseases that will not infect all mammals, only a few that are closely related."

"Yes," said Hackett, "but there are diseases that do cross those lines."

"And all of them originated on Earth. We have not had a single example of organisms developing on a different world, off Earth, that has caused any eruption of disease on Earth when they were transplanted to Earth either by accident on returning probes or in the scientific environment."

"But we've just come back from a very Earth-like environment," said Hackett.

"It was still a different world," said O'Neill.

"We have no real experience with this, do we?" said Hackett.

O'Neill took a deep breath and let it out slowly. He said, "We have explored a few worlds that were Earth-like back in the days of faster-than-light travel, and we have found some animal life on those worlds. The only real trouble we have had is that some substances that those animals tolerated, that those animals created for defense, were toxic to us, but those were chemical reactions and not disease."

"But your exposure was limited and your database, such as it was, was limited."

"Yes."

"Still you're satisfied that we don't need to make any special arrangements for the return of the fish tank or for the crew on those missions."

O'Neill looked helplessly at the others as if asking them for assistance. When no one spoke, he said, "We had the top biologists look into this question in depth, and they said there was no real danger to Earth-based life. I don't know what more we could do about it."

"A period of isolation?" suggested Hackett.

"For how long? What is the incubation period for the microbes that concern you? Some Earth diseases lie dormant for years, even decades. Would you have us suspend our operations now that we've finally got a system that works?"

Hackett shrugged.

"If no one else has any questions about this," said O'Neill pointedly, "we'll move on."

For the next twenty minutes they discussed their observations, but no one had much to say that hadn't been recorded in some fashion and transmitted from the fish tank back to the hangar and the control room. The preliminary study had been finished as those in the control room had watched everything on the various screens and displays.

Satisfied that they had finished, O'Neill stood and said, "We'll get you on the bus and back into the city in a few minutes. We'll have another meeting tomorrow unless there is something that needs to be discussed now."

No one said anything.

[2]

SITTING IN HIS APARTMENT, THE FLAT-SCREEN cycling as it ran through the channels, scanning from one to the next, Hackett still worried about the possibility of disease. What O'Neill said had made some sense to him, but something about it didn't seem quite right. He wished he had paid more attention to the biology classes he'd taken as a student, but then, he had been in those classes almost two hundred years ago. What he learned then had certainly been superseded by now.

Bakker, tired from her searches of the star fields and the debriefing, had gone into the bedroom and to sleep with hardly a word. Hackett had wanted to talk to her about microorganisms and contamination. Instead, he sat there, for an hour, letting the flat-screen cycle, hoping for something that would catch his attention. He kept telling himself he was going to get up and do something in a minute, but there was something hypnotic about the continuing slide of channels and his desire to do nothing.

Finally he pushed himself off the couch and walked into the kitchen for a glass of water. He drank that and returned to the living room, feeling apprehensive about something. It was a nondirectional worry, though he figured it had to do with the trip he had just taken and his concern about possible catastrophic contamination.

He sat down and switched on the mike so that he could access the Internet. He said, simply, "Biology."

When that database opened, he said, "Disease."

When that opened, he stopped, unsure how to proceed. There were millions of files, and he wasn't sure how to frame the next question. He wanted to know something about the development of disease and what disease would cross species lines and what wouldn't and why they wouldn't. He remembered reading or hearing about Ebola, which supposedly originally attacked only monkeys or apes, and there were strains of it that still infected only monkeys. In fact, some Ebola seemed to infect only chimpanzees and not any of the other apes.

Back in the late twentieth century, there had been an outbreak of Ebola in Reston, Virginia, among imported monkeys waiting in quarantine. The virus was airborne, something not seen in other strains of Ebola, and it killed the monkeys quickly. Fortunately, it didn't jump to humans, and the strain, at least in Reston, had been eradicated.

The frightening thing was that the virus had become airborne. Rather than being communicated from one individual to another by a mixing of bodily fluids, it had only required a common source of air. That meant, simply, that the monkeys in the same room with the infected individuals soon developed the disease, and those in other rooms that used the same ventilation system also got sick.

Maybe that was the place to begin his search. With Ebola and Reston. He spoke those two words into the search engine and waited. He read over a couple of reports and then realized that the question he wanted to ask actually involved extraterrestrial organisms. He took out *Ebola* and *Reston* and replaced them with *extraterrestrial*, *disease*, and *microorganisms*.

What he learned confirmed what O'Neill had told him. Given experiences on Earth, even when two species had common ancestors, it was difficult, if not impossible for them to reproduce. Germs, called pathogens, were normally species-specific. Rarely could they cross species lines. A disease that infected dogs wouldn't be passed to humans, and vice versa.

He learned there were exceptions, such as rabies, but rabies didn't infect reptiles. Toxins, injected by venomous snakes, often killed humans, but that was a chemical reaction and not a disease. The toxin had to be injected and in a few cases, merely "spit" at the victim as long as it could gain access to the bloodstream through open sources.

What it boiled down to was that all the research that had been conducted in the last two hundred years, and that included some microbes found high in the Earth's atmosphere and deep in the oceans near thermal vents and those that survived in the harsh environments on a moon of Jupiter and another on a moon of Neptune, had little relation to human life.

The limited evidence recovered and the suggestions of research on Earth said that creatures that evolved on different worlds would not cross-contaminate one another. Species on Earth that developed in isolation often could not contaminate one another. It was only after generations that evolution would produce creatures that could interact, meaning simply that pathogens could, after generations, evolve to the point where they could infect humans.

The possibility was there, but extremely remote. It was the reverse that concerned scientists the most. That is, human exploration would leave behind microscopic traces that would eventually evolve on those new worlds, creating havoc there. The danger to humans and Earth was limited, but the danger to those other worlds was great.

And then Hackett realized something else. The experiments were being conducted on Mars. The fish tank was sent on exploration from Mars and returned to Mars. If they brought back some kind of disease, assuming there wasn't an incubation period of months or years, the Martian population could be isolated from that of Earth. The disease could be contained on Mars without much danger to the populations of Earth or the populations on other worlds in the Solar System.

The bedroom door slid open, and Bakker appeared, looking tired, mussed, and unhappy. She looked up at the screen, saw the information about extraterrestrial pathogens, and glowered at Hackett.

"Just what in the hell are you doing?" she asked.

"Research."

"You find what you're looking for?"

Hackett spoke softly, and the screen faded away. He said, simply, "Yes."

"Then let's go to bed."

[3]

SALLY CLINTON, OLD BY EARTH STANDARDS A hundred years ago, but rather young by Martian standards, walked into the lab and watched the activity swirl around her. It was a large, white room, brightly lit, with a positive air pressure to keep contaminates at bay. It had an air lock system that would, in theory, keep the germs contained inside, if there was any sort of breakdown of the internal security.

Clinton had stopped outside the large air lock to don a white jumpsuit and to put white booties on her feet. She put on gloves and made sure that they were properly fastened to her wrists so that nothing could get inside to infect her, just as she had similarly secured the booties. She put on a hairnet and finished sealing herself into the suit before she entered the air lock and research room.

Those working inside, four men and two women, paid her no attention. They were examining the samples that had been brought back from the new world.

Clinton had been impressed with the outside protective preparations, though she thought of them as unnecessary.

Inside the research area, those procedures seemed to have broken down. No one was paying much attention to cross-contamination or keeping the various samples separated while they worked to analyze them. She even noticed a tear in one of the women's suits.

Clinton walked up to one of the work stations and watched as the young woman there analyzed a sample of what looked to be a drop of mud.

"Have you found anything?" asked Clinton.

The woman jumped slightly, startled, and then looked up at Clinton. "Microscopic life in the soil."

"Animal or vegetable?"

"I have some animal life here. Single cell and not very complex, but I believe it to be animal life. Nothing any larger than single cell."

Clinton nodded and pointed to a number of sample containers sitting opened nearby.

"Are you following protocol in dealing with these samples?" she asked.

"There is nothing to worry about. We know they all came from the same place, and weren't collected with all that much precision at the site. All I want to do is make an effort to stop cross-contamination among them here, but it's probably too late even for that."

Clinton didn't like that answer, but she wasn't sure what might be wrong with it, given the haphazard way the samples had been collected and recovered and then transported to the lab. It was her responsibility to ensure that lab procedures were not violated. The collection techniques in the field were someone else's concern.

On the other hand, the technicians were highly trained and knew what they were doing. They had practiced these

things for years and had even done them for real when the
first of the microbes had been found on Titan not all that
long ago, so they had some practical experience.

Ignoring, for the moment, the protocol violations, Clinton asked, "You're sure you have animals in the soil?"

"On a microscopic level, yes. I haven't found any traces
of larger animals, though."

"Meaning?"

"No hair, no feces, nothing other than single-cell creatures, at least in these samples. Of course, that, in and of itself might not be significant."

Clinton nodded and moved on. She watched other re-
searchers examine samples and enter their observations
into computer spreadsheets to be shared with other scientists on Mars and on Earth. They could engage in real-time
chats, as if they were all in the same room, on the same
planet, looking at the same samples. The only thing the
others couldn't do, meaning those watching through the
computer networks, was prepare the slides themselves, but
only because the equipment that would allow them to do
that hadn't been connected. Had they needed the capability, it wouldn't have taken long to set it up.

Clinton wandered around the room for nearly an hour,
surveying the procedures but not interfering. She would
stop and watch and then move on.

Finally tired, and just a little bored, she walked toward
the air lock to leave. One of the male technicians, an older
man who was the brightest of the techs, approached her
cautiously. He looked around, as if expecting to find
someone spying on them, and then leaned in close.

"I've found something that bothers me."

"Yes?"

Again he looked around and then whispered. "I have found some DNA in the samples."

"So what?"

"In our searches of extraterrestrial biological samples, limited though it has been, we didn't find DNA. Their basic building blocks did not include DNA as we define it. Yeah, there were amino acids, but not DNA."

"Are you saying that these samples are of Earth-based life?"

The technician looked pained, as if he was going to be sick. He shook his head and said, "I'm not sure what it means, but I have found DNA."

Clinton grinned and waved a hand, indicating the whole lab. "You contaminated your sample."

Before he could protest, she added quickly, "Or someone in here contaminated it. Or the explorers inadvertently contaminated it as they were collecting it or transporting it back while in the fish tank."

For a moment the technician was quiet, then he said, "I don't think so. I think I've found DNA in these samples, and that means we might have a problem with diseases. We might want to rethink the way we're gathering this stuff. We might want to rethink our isolation protocols."

Clinton took a deep breath and was going to say something sharp or dismissive but thought better of it. Maybe there was a problem and she should examine it. After all that was her main function. She couldn't just blow off the concern without making an effort to learn a little more about it.

"Be careful with the rest of your samples and get me the complete results as soon as you can."

She looked at the others working in the lab and realized

that the secret couldn't be contained, if a secret it was. Too many outside observers and too much information being posted just as quickly as it was found.

"Be a little circumspect in the results you post," said Clinton, quietly, "but don't act guilty, it'll just call attention to you."

"What am I supposed to do?"

"Complete your work, check it carefully, and get those results to me as soon as you can. Answer any questions put to you, unless they begin to dance around this DNA problem, and then refer them to me."

The technician looked visibly relieved with the instruction. He nodded and hurried back to his workstation.

Clinton opened the air lock and stepped into the chamber to remove her outer garments, gloves, and booties. She hadn't liked what she had heard but wasn't sure that it was quite as important as the technician had thought. Amino acids had been found in meteorites and in comets, so maybe, on some distant worlds, DNA, or structures similar had developed as life developed. A great deal of work at the molecular level was needed before anyone began to panic.

CHAPTER 12

[1]

THE FIRST JOURNEY TO A NEW WORLD USING the fish tank with a living crew had been a rousing success, according to what everyone said. They had found a pleasant planet filled with plant life, and the planet would require little if any modification for human habitation. It was a pristine world that had no pollution, no indigenous intelligent life-forms, and no large, dangerous predators.

Other studies, completed on the samples brought back by that crew, showed no microscopic life that would cause humans trouble on the world. They now had an environment where they could adapt and reproduce, provided they could find the necessary elements for their survival.

Bakker had been unable to locate anything in the star fields that was familiar, though there were lots of stars visible and the photographs were better than she had hoped for. Though she said that the journey must have been farther than anticipated or they were looking in the wrong place for the familiar patterns in the night sky, she didn't really believe the trip had been all that far so she stepped up her efforts to find something familiar to help her identify the star system.

So now they had a success, where the voyagers returned as healthy as they had been when they left. They had found an interesting but nonhostile world that had nearly everything they needed to survive. They had found the perfect place for humans to colonize, though none of the travelers had thought in those terms.

After two weeks, which Hackett didn't believe to be sufficient to review everything gathered during the journey, they sat again in the conference room planning another voyage.

Pictures from the next target's surface hovered above the conference table, sliding from one view into the next like an old-fashioned slide projector set on automatic. It wasn't an area of a planet that was heavily forested, but more of a savannah, like the Great Plains of the United States, with some distant trees.

"A little different this time," said O'Neill, somewhat unnecessarily.

"Signs of animal life?" asked Hackett.

"This time, yes. Some large animals that we believe to be herbivores. And something like birds, though none of them got close enough to the cameras for us to make an identification, even with increased magnification. They were in the sky, flying, but then, bats do that, too."

"And no sign of intelligent life?" asked Bakker.

"Around the landing site, no."

"Meaning there are indications?" asked Hackett.

O'Neill hesitated, and then said, "No. Not really."

Hackett laughed and asked, "What does *not really* mean?"

"We've gotten off on a tangent here," said O'Neill. "It's not something that we need to discuss now. Wait for the biologist to provide the data."

"Seems to me," said Hackett, "that if there is an indigenous sentient species, there is no need to continue the discussion. We need to avoid that world."

O'Neill held up a hand like a policeman directing traffic on a busy street. He said, "Let's go on to the other matters until Doctor Curry arrives. He'll fill you in."

Clark, who had remained silent, looked up from the notes he had taken on his PDA and said, "It's a dry world?"

"The area we'll be landing is drier than the last one. More like the Great Plains on Earth. Enough moisture for a variety of plant life, but not wet enough for swamps and jungle. Warm, but not hot and humid."

"You base this solely on the pictures you have here?" asked Clark.

"And the temperature readings we've gotten as well. We have some weather data available, though weather data gathered over only a few hours might not be representative of this new world's weather patterns."

Hackett said, "What I really want to do is make sure we're going to take weapons."

"Now wait a minute," said Cheney. "We shouldn't be exploring worlds where we need weapons. I didn't like it the last time."

"What about snakes?" asked Hackett.

"I don't know of a snake I couldn't outrun. And if it's

already bitten me, then a weapon isn't going to do me any good," said Cheney, seriously.

"Large carnivores?" asked Hackett.

O'Neill said, "Then we're back into another discussion. I doubt that any carnivore encountered would recognize you as a source of food."

"Unless they're territorial, as many carnivores are, and would attack because we're in their territory and they view us as a competitor. What if it thinks we're threatening its young?"

O'Neill suddenly looked very tired. He took a deep breath and said, "We have no indications of any large, territorial carnivores on this world. We have very limited information, which is why we want to explore."

Langston, who had been sitting quietly, listening to the debate finally spoke. "I wonder why, if you can gather all this data using robots and remote viewing, you need us to go to the new world."

"If you are unhappy with your assignment," snapped O'Neill, "you are welcome to quit at any time. Leave when you're ready."

"It was only a question," said Langston.

"And a necessary one," said Cheney.

"Okay. The same thing was said about space exploration, but we still put people into rockets and fired them to the moon and Mars and the outer worlds. You can only predict so many scenarios before something unexpected comes up—"

"Yes," said Langston, interrupting, "but you have direct communication with the fish tank and seem to be directing the robots. Why do people have to go?"

O'Neill was silent for a moment, thinking about the reasons for sending people through in the fish tank. It had nothing to do with exploration. It served as a limited test of the environmental living conditions on the new world and human reaction to it. The test was something needed, because numbers and samples didn't always tell the whole story.

Of course, he could always say that they had to go because those were the orders, and while that might work with a strictly military team, it wouldn't work with civilians. They wanted answers to their questions.

It wasn't as if he had complete information. The pressure on him was coming from those he worked with, but only because they were getting pressure from a higher level. He'd met with Pierce, Travis, Gettman, and Griffin, of course, but they didn't share everything they knew with him. He suspected there was a good reason for sending in people rather than engaging in remote investigation, but wasn't sure what it was.

Thinking about it, he wondered if aliens might be on their way back to the Solar System. Last time the aliens had passed them by, as if they had a mission more important that meeting with another race. Maybe this time they were coming to make that contact.

Of course, he didn't know that. He didn't know much of anything, other than that the pressure was on. Results were desired, so he passed that pressure on down the line.

So, he said, "Because, sometimes the remote controls and the robotics just aren't adequate for a situation. Sometimes we need the flexibility that a human on the scene can provide. Sometimes we need the intuition of the human mind, and sometimes we need the infinitely detailed observations that only a human being can make."

That answer seemed to satisfy them for the moment, but O'Neill knew that if they thought about it carefully, they would realize that the real-time link allowed for all those things without a human on the scene.

Hackett asked, "When do you plan to send us?"

O'Neill looked at his watch. "Planning to be completed in two days with the first journey set for one week. Now if we can get back to the briefing."

[2]

CLARK, WITH BEKKA CHENEY AND STEPHEN Novotny, left the briefing more than a little annoyed. They walked out into the Martian evening, as the dusk seemed to blend into the night. Lights were on all over the city, adding their glow to the atmosphere and hiding some of the dimmer stars. From the city, neither of Mars's moons could be seen. They were dimly glowing hunks of rock, captured asteroids really, that didn't seem to qualify as actual satellites. They flashed across the night, when visible, and didn't cast much in the way of light.

"Where are we going?" asked Novotny.

"Anywhere far away from O'Neill and the institute," said Clark.

"I guess I don't know why you're so mad about this," said Novotny.

Clark stopped walking and looked right at him.

"You sat in there," said Clark, "and listened to everything that he said. It makes no sense. We could do everything they want remotely from the control room. There's no reason to send us out on these missions."

Cheney didn't like that. She wanted to believe that she was doing something important, something that few others could do, and now Clark was saying that it wasn't important at all. Technicians in a control room could do it with robots. Which made them just robots, with a little more circuitry and a few more responses.

"What if some problem arises on the new world that they can't figure out in a control room?"

"What would that be, Bekka? You've got human operators right there, looking at the scene in real time. They are controlling the robots if necessary. They're gathering the samples. The controllers can order anything they want."

"There is nothing like having a real person on the site," she said.

"Which we have," said Clark. "No, there is something else going on here that they're not telling us."

"And what would that be?" asked Novotny.

Clark started walking again, moving toward the downtown center, where they would be with other people and have a little background noise. And where he could point them into a bistro or a club. "I don't know."

"Look," said Cheney, "we sent men to the moon in the middle of the twentieth century for no other reason than to prove that we could. Those men did nothing that even the limited robotics of the time couldn't do."

"So what's your point?" asked Clark.

Cheney shrugged. "No point, I guess, just a statement. It was done because we could do it."

"Nope," said Clark. "The oldsters put people at risk because they didn't care about the risks. They were doing something that hadn't been done before, because they had few options. But there really is no reason for us to make these journeys now. There is something else going on."

"Then I ask again, What?" said Novotny.

"I don't know, but I want to find out."

"And if you can't find out, what are you going to do about it?" asked Novotny. "Refuse to go?"

"No. I'd rather be on the inside looking out than on the outside looking in. Besides, I have a better chance of learning what's really going on if I'm on the inside running around. I like being on the inside."

Novotny pointed to a sign ahead and asked, "You want to get a drink in there?"

Cheney shook her head. "I think I want to head back to the apartment. It's been a long day."

Clark said, "One drink won't hurt us. Maybe we can come up with a reason."

"No," said Cheney. "I don't really care what the reason is. I have a good job, one with an important mission. I'm not sitting at a computer or worrying about some trivial problem. I have something important to do."

"If you want to believe that," said Clark.

Now she stopped walking and turned to face him. She felt the anger boil in the pit of her stomach, and it was almost as if she wanted to hit him. Slap his smug face.

"That's exactly what I believe," said Cheney. "Money has been spent. Piles of it. People have worked long and hard to provide us with this opportunity. Now we can actually reach the stars, a promise that was made long ago. This is something important for all of us."

Clark started to speak, but Cheney cut him off.

"No, I don't want to hear any more of your cynicism. I don't want to hear any more of your conspiracy theories.

Sometimes people just act out of altruism and a desire to do something that hasn't been done before. Not everyone thinks like you do."

"Those in power always think exactly like I do," said Clark, sarcastically.

Cheney ignored that, but she knew that all too often he was right. Those with power often used it, not for the benefit of humanity, but for their own personal gain. But this was different. She couldn't see how those in power would benefit.

[3]

O'NEILL LEFT THE MEETING MORE THAN UN-happy. He was used to the youngsters accepting all that he said as if it was the gospel. He didn't like the challenges, especially when he didn't have a good answer for them.

When he entered the conference room, he found Clinton, Curry, and Davis already there. Sitting at the head of the table was Anderson Thomas, the man with two last names, who was known as either Tom or Andy, depending on when you met him or the time of the day. He changed names periodically to keep everyone on their toes. He was older than O'Neill and was the overall chairman of the traveling committee.

He waited for O'Neill to sit down and said, "I have looked at everything from the new world and see no reason that we can't begin the project now."

O'Neill took a deep breath. He didn't like confrontation, and he knew that this conversation was headed to one. There was no way to avoid it.

"You've looked at everything carefully?" asked O'Neill.

"Dick, I said that I had."

"I have a report that DNA was found on the new world, and I can't see where we have had the time to fully research that problem."

"Why do you call it a problem?"

O'Neill looked to the others for support, but he didn't get it. They sat quietly, looking at the holographic displays or pretending they had found something fascinating on the floor or on the walls, or even in the holograph. O'Neill knew that he was on his own this time.

"While I'm not schooled in all the ramifications of this discovery, I seem to remember being told that an alien life-form would not have DNA as its basis, and if that were true, then we had real worry about cross-contamination with our human populations. However—"

Thomas waved a hand to cut him off. "I believe that the sample was contaminated."

"Possibly, but why hurry?"

"I thought we had discussed this before. We need to move humanity out of the Solar System to prevent a catastrophe that would lead to our extinction."

O'Neill laughed. "Yes, but is the sun about to go nova and no one told me?"

"Sarcasm is the lowest form of humor," said Thomas icily.

"I thought that was the pun," said Curry.

"This is not a discussion of literary tradition," snapped Thomas. "It is a discussion of our next move, and I want to begin the selection process for the migration."

"Until we have looked a little deeper," said O'Neill, "I'm opposed. We have no need to rush."

"Then why are you launching another voyage?" asked Thomas. He smiled as if he had caught O'Neill in a contradiction, forgetting that the launch schedule had been created by his committee and given to O'Neill.

"Because we don't want to put all our eggs in one basket," said O'Neill. "We're supposed to identify a number of planets that will support human life."

Davis, who had remained quiet, finally spoke. "I thought that was the purpose of the Generation Ships. Break humanity free of the Solar System."

"Okay, smart guy," said Thomas, "please tell me the status of those ships."

"Out of the Solar System and moving among the stars searching for new worlds to populate."

"When was the last time there was any communication with them? What was that communication?"

"The point," said O'Neill, "is that we have already moved humanity, in a limited fashion, out of the Solar System."

"If those ships have not been destroyed, or if the populations on them haven't perished. And you are presupposing that they will find inhabitable planets before those closed systems collapse, as they eventually will."

"There is no reason to believe that those missions failed," said Davis.

"And no reason to suppose they have succeeded either," said Thomas.

"But it also suggests that we have no reason to hurry, not to mention that the human race has survived for nearly ten million years without extinction," said O'Neill.

"We need to create a sense of urgency," said Thomas. "We need to get people moving, because if we rely on your attitude, people will still be arguing about it when a catastrophe does fall on them."

"What form is this catastrophe going to take?" asked Clinton. Like O'Neill, she was not privy to the secrets of the higher committee.

Figuring that he could create a sense of urgency without revealing anything that they knew, Thomas said, "Let me remind you that there have been six events in the history of the Solar System that nearly destroyed all life on Earth."

"Damn, Andy," said O'Neill, "those were not overnight events, and they only involved a single planet. We're spread throughout the system, and any disaster on Earth would not affect us here on Mars. And the more likely catastrophe here would certainly not affect the Earth."

"Disease can spread among the planets and all the outposts in the Solar System," said Thomas as a way of diverting the conversation to a safer subject.

"Again," said O'Neill, "do you know something that you're not telling us?"

"No, of course not. But I want to get this project going. I want to have people working hard to finish some of it before something sneaks up on us. If a catastrophe does strike, we'll be able to survive it."

"Okay," said O'Neill, "but I don't know what I could do to speed things up."

"Review more worlds," said Thomas. "Train additional teams. There is no reason that we must be limited to a single team or a single voyage."

"Actually," said O'Neill, "unless we build another fish tank, we *are* limited to one voyage at a time."

"Then build it," snapped Thomas. He stood up. "I want to hear about some progress in a week."

CHAPTER 13

[1]

THERE WAS NO REASON FOR THE TIME FRAME to have been constricted, thought Hackett. There was no reason that he could see for a sudden increase in activity or for the laid-back nature of the original missions to be changed.

But Hackett was a military officer, and the assumption in the military was always that those with the higher ranks were smarter than those of the lesser ranks. The definition of *smarter* in this case was "more experienced." Those who had been in the military longer were older and more experienced. They had been around long enough to make mistakes, see the mistakes of others, and learn from all of that. So, when the pace of the exploration increased, Hackett assumed, reluctantly, that those in charge of the project, who by his definition had learned from experience, knew what they were doing.

Hackett had also been around long enough to understand what *assume* meant so that he wasn't beyond asking questions. Sometimes he did it quietly, trying not to upset anyone, just gathering information. Other times he did it confrontationally, because, if he did it any other way, he wouldn't get any answers to his questions.

So, he went to find O'Neill. He took Bakker along, because she was part of the project, he knew her very well, and she understood science. She often thought of questions to ask that he hadn't thought of, and she had a different set of beliefs and perspectives to use in asking. She understood some things he didn't, and she could help him later.

They found O'Neill in his city office, on the ground floor of a massive building that was somehow reminiscent of a pyramid but had sleeker and more delicate lines. The sides were sharply sloped, so that the building rose high, without the massive base that would be expected on a pyramid constructed using the conventional methods.

They entered through a door that was made of air and into a lobby that was huge, open, bright, nearly bare of furniture, and without a receptionist. If there was security, it was hidden somewhere, probably concealed out of sight in the wall decorations and behind doors.

They crossed the lobby, and no one or nothing stopped them. They pushed through a double door at the far end and into a maze of hallways and cubicles. They could hear noise rising from some of them and occasionally saw people as they moved about on their business. No one took notice of them, and no one offered to help them.

"Some things never change," said Bakker. "You'd think

they'd at least be curious enough to ask us who we are rather than letting us walk around in here unescorted."

"But when you do that," said Hackett, "then you own the problem. It's easier to pretend that everyone is where he or she is supposed to be and knows what's happening rather than ask a question and end up as the guide."

"So, what do we do?"

"Look for private offices and see what or who we can find," he said.

They moved through the open, cubicle area and down one of the hallways. But unlike two hundred years earlier, the offices weren't identified with names or titles, but instead with pictures. It was the natural extension of the early twenty-first century, where identification had evolved from the written name, understandable only to those who could read, to pictures that everyone could recognize. There were no braille characters, because blindness had been nearly eradicated on Earth and there were no blind people on Mars.

They walked down the hallway, looking at pictures of the occupants of the offices until they came to the end of the corridor. There, on a massive double door was a picture of O'Neill. And like those pictures of earlier years on Earth, it had been defaced slightly by the addition of a pointed beard and two horns, giving it a comical rather than demonic appearance. Some things just never changed.

There was no knob on the door, but it opened when they approached it.

"Either someone was watching," said Hackett, "or it has a photoelectric cell."

"If it opens for everyone, then it kind of loses its purpose as a door."

Inside was another open space with two black leather chairs, a coffee table with nothing on it, and a large desk for a receptionist. No one was sitting there. It was the typical office waiting room, the style of which hadn't changed in more than two hundred years either.

O'Neill opened one of the side doors and came out. He grinned broadly and said, "I've been expecting you."

That took Hackett by surprise. "We didn't have an appointment."

"Well, no, but I knew when we announced the upswing in our tempo, you'd want to talk about it, even if you hadn't come here in your capacity as director of the Galaxy Exploration Team."

He waved them into his office, which was different. There was no desk, only a reclining chair set back from the wall that held the flat-screen. There was no indication of a keyboard, and no signs of any research files. Everything was electronically stored for ease of retrieval and was voice-activated. A person could just sit there and atrophy while watching the flat-screen and asking for information that was provided through the various electronic connections.

There were two other chairs, arranged so that whoever sat in them could see the flat-screen. If the recliner was swiveled around all those in the office could engage in face-to-face conversation. There were no other furnishings.

Once they were all seated, with O'Neill facing them, in his chair that was positioned slightly above theirs, his fingers tented under his chin, he asked, "What can I do for you?"

Hackett shot a glance at Bakker and then, without preamble asked, "Why the sudden push for exploration?"

"I'm not sure that we have a sudden push," responded O'Neill. "Just a desire to make full use of our assets now that we understand their capabilities."

"Okay," said Hackett, nodding but not believing. "Now what's the real story here."

"I'm afraid that I don't understand."

"You said that you expected me to show up, because I'm head of the Galaxy Exploration Team. You have accelerated the research package so that your fish tank is going out on another mission almost immediately. Why the sudden pressure?"

O'Neill was quiet for a moment and then said, "There really is no pressure. We have expended a lot of time, money, and effort in creating the fish tank and the process to force it to travel to new worlds. We're just trying to make efficient use of that asset. That's all."

Hackett turned and looked at Bakker, waiting for her to say something. Hackett said nothing and let the silence among them build.

Finally he said, "If we make good use of the natural resources on the asteroids, mine the moons of the larger planets, then we have enough resources to last for thousands of years, probably millions of years. There is no pressing need to get out of the system."

O'Neill shrugged. He didn't have an answer that he could share with them. He wasn't sure what they expected him to say, so he said nothing.

The silence grew thick again. Hackett knew it was a good interrogation technique. The idea that the subject would become so uncomfortable in the silence that he would blurt out something incriminating eventually. All it took was some patience on the part of the interrogator.

Finally O'Neill said, "Pressure from above to make the project pay for itself quickly, I suppose. Too much spent with no real return."

Hackett wasn't sure that he believed that. The one thing he had seen was that very little on Mars resulted in monetary worries. On the contrary, Mars, it seemed, was a vast tub of money, and there was very little in the way of corporate pressure to produce a profit. Mars was more like a governmental agency that handed out money for research, with little in the way of an expected return. Or, an expected short-term return.

O'Neill, however, having heard the sound of his own words, almost believed some of it. Without thinking about it much, he added, "We've spent a lot of money on the research, and our sponsors want to see some of that money back."

Hackett asked, "Aren't we in danger of spending more by accelerating the process? What if someone gets killed?"

"No one's going to get killed," said O'Neill. He grinned and asked, "Is there anything else?"

"This doesn't make any sense to me," said Hackett. "There must be something else going on here, behind the scenes."

"There isn't."

O'Neill fell silent for a moment and then grinned with sudden inspiration. "We broke the light barrier, if you will. We can travel interstellar distances without worry about time dilation. We can explore the stars. That has been a dream of humanity from the moment they understood what the stars were."

"Yeah?" said Hackett.

"No one crossed the Atlantic for centuries, other than some Vikings and then, suddenly, Columbus reports on a new world and everyone wants to go. We have the same thing here. We do it now because we can."

"I'm not sure I find that sufficient," said Hackett. "At least not for accelerating the schedule."

"Well, there you have it anyway," said O'Neill sitting forward.

"There has to be an underlying reason for the acceleration of the schedule. What you have said doesn't make sense."

O'Neill fell back and said, "There are those who worry that we're using up our resources too fast. They want to ensure a continuing supply. Travel now is somewhat costly, and we don't know what we'll find. By the time we have that worked out, we'll be ready to exploit the finds."

Hackett shook his head. "Nope. I simply don't believe that."

"There's nothing more that I can tell you."

Hackett sat quietly for a moment, digesting the information. Finally he nodded and looked at Bakker. "You have anything to ask?"

Bakker shook her head and Hackett said, "I guess not."

They left together and when they got into the corridor, away from O'Neill's office, Bakker said, "Wasn't that the biggest load of crap you ever heard?"

Hackett didn't think it was the biggest, but it was certainly in the top two.

[2]

THEY ASSEMBLED IN THE HANGAR LATE IN THE
day. For reasons Hackett didn't understand, that was the
time the mission had been scheduled. The fish tank stood
in the center, looking as if it had been modified in the short
time he had been away from the hangar. It seemed bigger
somehow, and looked as if the glass had been reinforced.

Clark and his team stood in a line near the fish tank, facing it, almost like a military unit formed for a briefing before a mission. The line was straight, and they weren't
talking to one another.

Hackett and Bakker approached, but didn't join the line.
They stood behind it, waiting with the others.

O'Neill left the control room and walked across the
hangar, his footsteps echoing from the walls. That surprised Hackett. He would have expected soft shoes and
sound-deadening material inside the hangar.

O'Neill stopped in front of them and said, "This is be-
coming routine. No need for any sort of pep talk, I suspect.
You all know what's going on and what's going to happen.
Are there any new questions?"

When no one raised a hand, O'Neill said, "Well, then,
let's get set. I think we'll launch this in a few minutes."

Clark was the first to move. He walked toward the hatch
and opened it. He stepped through and took the chair closest to it. He strapped himself in as the others climbed
through the hatch and prepared themselves for the trip.
This time, the entire crew was going, including Bakker.

Once they were all inside the fish tank and strapped in,
the crew in the control room began the countdown. Hackett found himself staring at the bundle of weapons, hoping

that they would function properly and wondering why he hadn't been asked to inspect them before the trip. Civilians didn't understand the importance of weapons in what could be a hostile environment. The best scenario was not to need them, but if they were needed, they had to work perfectly.

But even as he thought about that, he realized the countdown had reached zero and he was suddenly dizzy. It was exactly the same sensation that he had felt at the beginning of the other trip.

He glanced over at Bakker. Her face was washed out, bright, and white, but Hackett didn't know if that was a result of the sudden and bizarre lighting or if she was about to be sick. He spoke to her, but his words seemed to come out in slow motion and in a deep voice that didn't sound right even to him. It was almost as if he could see the words coming from his mouth and bouncing off her ears, like they might with a cartoon character. She turned to look at him and grinned weakly.

And then, as before, the trip ended with the hangar gone and them sitting on a low hill with gentle, grassy slopes. There was a line of trees maybe a mile away, which looked like they might be growing along the bank of a river. Overhead a creature that looked remarkably like a cardinal wheeled on the wind, almost as if inspecting them. Higher, in the sky were puffy clouds that suggested a warm, summer afternoon.

Hackett seemed to recover first and asked, "Is everyone all right?"

Clark nodded, and Bakker said, her voice shaky, "I'm fine. That's quite a ride."

Hackett stood up and moved toward the hatch. They already knew that the atmosphere was breathable, so he opened the hatch and stepped through. He wasn't thinking about claiming the world or naming it as the first human to set foot on it. He just wanted to get out of the fish tank.

It was beginning to smell. Someone had gotten sick.

[3]

WITH BAKKER, CHENEY, AND NOVOTNY, HACK-ett, carrying one of the rifles almost like a hunter in a nineteenth-century African safari, had walked down to the trees. They hadn't seen much in the way of animal life in the short time they had been in the new world, but they knew it existed. They had seen the bird, had seen insects, and had heard distant cries of animals. One of them sounded almost like a lion announcing his ownership of the territory.

They reached the river that looked to be a hundred yards across, five or six feet deep, and as clear as the stream that he had seen on the last trip. Fish could be seen in the water, some of them about six feet long, looking like the giant channel catfish of Earth.

"This is strange," said Bakker. "This looks exactly like Earth."

"Parallel evolution?" asked Cheney. "I mean, the conditions on this world are similar to those found on Earth. Wouldn't the animal and plant life tend to develop along the same lines, given the same environmental conditions?"

"I wouldn't think so," said Bakker. "The odds are too small for that."

Hackett crouched near the riverbank and watched the

fish swimming just under the surface. Some looked like trout, some looked like pike, and there were the huge catfish at the bottom of the river.

Novotny sat down, his back to a tree.

"Sure looks like Earth," said Hackett.

"But, of course, it's not," said Bakker. "If it was Earth, then we'd see signs of civilization, not a huge, open savannah without any indications of human life."

"Southern Africa?" said Hackett. "Or South America? Argentina?"

"With the roaring we heard, I'd have to say Africa," said Cheney.

"But there isn't anyplace like this on Earth," said Bakker, "and probably hasn't been for five hundred years."

Hackett sat down, the rifle across his lap. He looked up into the deep blue of the sky, broken by the fluffy cottonlike clouds that sure looked like those on Earth. He thought, he could see a thunderhead building in the distance.

"I don't like this," said Bakker. "There is something wrong here, but I don't understand it."

"What could be wrong?" asked Cheney.

"This just doesn't feel right."

Hackett laughed and said, "We're in no danger here. There are no signs of intelligent life and no signs of civilization. We should be able to protect ourselves."

"That's not what I'm thinking about," said Bakker.

Hackett took a deep breath, held it, and then sighed deeply. "This is a beautiful place."

"Yes, but where is it?" asked Bakker.

"That's for you to figure out," said Hackett.

"I think I already know, and you're not going to like it."

[4]

WHEN IT WAS CLEAR TO EVERYONE IN THE CON-trol room that the fish tank had landed safely on the savannah of the new world, O'Neill quietly slipped from the hangar. He walked out, into the mild Martian afternoon, into the dim glow of the middle of the day, and then strolled toward the bus.

It was parked fifty feet from the entrance to the hangar. The driver, an older man with stooped shoulders brought on by bone disease that had somehow missed the geneticists, was sitting on one of the steps. When he spotted O'Neill he got to his feet. In another time, on another planet, he would have been smoking.

As he approached, O'Neill said, "The others will be here for quite a while and won't be needing transportation. Will you run me into the city?"

"Of course," said the driver, climbing up into the bus and behind the control panel.

O'Neill didn't want to get involved in a discussion with the man, so he moved toward the rear of the bus and sat down on a long bench seat. He leaned back and looked out the window at a landscape that was desolate. Red dust that stretched toward the horizon, with the hint of an escarpment miles away, but no signs of life. He knew that most of that was the rim of a huge meteor crater. The Martian surface, without water, didn't weather craters as readily as the Earth.

The bus pulled away from the hangar, turned toward the afternoon sun, which didn't blind the way it would on Earth. They drove along the magnetic bed of the roadway, picking up speed as they moved.

When they reached the city, the driver turned toward the headquarters building and stopped outside. O'Neill stood, moved down the aisle, and laid a hand on the driver's shoulder. "Thanks. I'll be about an hour, and then I'll need to go back out to the hangar."

"What if the others need to come into the city?"

"That's not going to happen for a while. They'll be watching the experiment until long after dark and will probably stay there overnight. You can wait here."

"Yes, sir."

O'Neill walked into the building, through the deserted lobby, beyond the doors that led into the bullpen area of cubicles, and through more doors that led to a long corridor. His office was at the far end, but he stopped short, entering a conference room about halfway down.

Sitting at a long oval table in a pit-like area were several people, including Bruce Pierce and Nancy Travis, who held the oversight on the interstellar program.

"Please, have a seat," said Pierce. He didn't bother to introduce the others. O'Neill knew who they were, anyway, had spoken to them on occasion, but wasn't friends with any of them. They were the ruling group who only came out to the hangar on rare occasions, but usually stayed in the city and who had little time for the "working" class.

O'Neill took his seat and waited.

A colored ball of light appeared over the table, hovered there momentarily, and grew into a scene of a grass-covered savannah where the fish tank now sat.

"That the new world?" asked Pierce.

"Yes."

"Have there been any signs of civilization or intelligent life anywhere on that world?"

"No. There is animal life on it, but we don't have a good sample of what to expect. We haven't seen enough of it to make a real determination."

"Dangerous?"

O'Neill looked at the man who had asked that question. A really old man, even by Martian standards. His skin looked like processed leather. He was nearly hairless with small tufts near his larger than normal ears. He looked like the pictures of Egyptian mummies O'Neill had seen. O'Neill didn't know his name and hadn't seen him before.

"We haven't had people there long enough to be certain. There are indications of some large animal life but we don't know if it is dangerous. Besides, some of the deadliest animals on Earth are very small."

"When will it be safe to start sending people through for colonization?"

O'Neill turned to look at the old man, the question on his face. He said, "I know the purpose here has been colonization. I know that we are interested in pushing the human race out of the Solar System, but, frankly, I don't understand the need to move this rapidly."

Pierce, still smiling benignly, asked, "Have you communicated this lackadaisical attitude to your team?"

"No. I have tried to build a sense of urgency in them, though I don't know why it is suddenly so important. There have been some questions about that."

"It's because we have developed the capability for interstellar travel and we want to begin the colonization," said Travis.

O'Neill took a deep breath, stared right at her, and said,

"I'm sorry, but I don't buy that. If we were worried about the continued existence of the human race, well, we have the Generation Ships pushing humans out into the galaxy. If we are only worried about colonization, then our early attempts at faster-than-light travel would be adequate. Our concern was that the returning crews came back to worlds they didn't know, so we found a way to fix that. What you are doing now makes no sense to me at all."

Pierce looked at the old man who sat quietly, his lips pursed. Finally he nodded once.

"All right," said Bruce, "the simple explanation is that we are now in competition for the best planets in our section of the galaxy. We want to establish a human presence on them as quickly as we can to deny them to our competitors."

O'Neill rocked back in his chair, surprised. He wasn't overly surprised by the announcement of a competitor, because he had known about that all his adult life. It was the plural that caught him by surprise. *Competitors.*

CHAPTER 14

[1]

IT WAS SO RELAXING BY THE STREAM, QUIET, warm, pleasant, that Hackett wasn't sure that he ever wanted to move. He could stay right there, watch the fish swim, watch the distant birds soar on the air currents and thermals, and remain happy. There was no imperative for him to move. Even the periodic roars from unseen beasts didn't disturb him.

Bakker walked over, looked down at him, and asked, "Shouldn't we head back?"

"Why?"

"Get there before dark."

Hackett looked up at the sun, which was sitting about midway between zenith and horizon, and said, "There'll be sunlight for a long time yet."

"Still," said Bakker.

Reluctantly Hackett pushed himself up and took a deep breath of the sweet air. "I could learn to really like it here. Pristine."

"Maybe you can retire here when that time comes," she said.

The roar came again, this time closer. Hackett looked in the direction of the sound, but could see nothing other than a gently sloping hill.

"That can't be a lion," said Hackett. "Sounds like it, but can't be."

"How do you know what a lion sounds like?"

"Been watching the Nature Channel again. Did you know that the lion roars actually had meaning—"

"Yeah, yeah," said Bakker. "We've known that for two hundred years. You finally catching up?"

Hackett shrugged. "I didn't spend my college years in the biology lab."

"Neither did I. I just pay attention."

They turned and walked up the hill toward the fish tank. One or two of the others were sitting in the grass near it, studying something on the ground between them. The others were scattered around the hillside.

As Hackett and Bakker approached, Jenny Langston waved them over. She pointed at something on the ground between her and Ralph Stepkowski.

Hackett stopped short. It looked like a gigantic dragonfly with a wingspan of nearly a yard. The body was glowing brightly, an iridescent blue green, depending on exactly how the light hit it.

"Liz shot it," said Langston. "I think she only wanted to stun it, but I think she killed it."

"I don't like this," said Bakker.

"Dragonflies are harmless," said Langston. "At least to humans."

"I'm not worried about that," said Bakker. "It's one more proof."

"Proof of what?" asked Hackett.

"I'd rather not say yet," said Bakker, "but I'm beginning to think that we've been misled."

Before he could ask the next question, Clark and Cheney walked toward them. Clark called out a greeting.

When they were close and could see the dragonfly, he said, "There's a swamp on the other side of the hill. Place is thick with those dragonflies and a bunch of other things. I saw a spider-like creature that was even bigger than that dragonfly. Had a head the size of a basketball."

Hackett was aware of the continuing roars from the other side of the river. He asked, "You see anything larger? Anything mammalian?"

Cheney laughed. "I don't know what could be worse than a spider so big that you'd have to shoot instead of step on it."

Hackett looked at her and asked, "What do you know about spiders? You were born on Mars."

"I've seen pictures, and I once went to Earth. I saw some very small ones there."

"I'd like to identify what is doing all the roaring," said Hackett.

Bakker said, "Given the way these things work, it's probably some little creature running around trying to scare everything else."

"It's working on me," said Cheney.

Clark said, "Why don't we get the dragonfly properly collected?"

"Meaning?"

"Put it in a sample container."

As Langston got to her feet to go into the fish tank, Hackett turned to Bakker. He asked quietly, "You have any idea where we are?"

"Yeah, I think I do. I see the clues around here, but I'm going to have to gather some additional data so that I can pinpoint things."

"You want to give me a hint?"

"I think you'll figure it out soon enough." She hesitated and then added again. "You won't like it."

[2]

THE FIRST NIGHT ON THE NEW PLANET WAS somewhat frightening, because no one knew what to expect. They had seen some huge insects, and they had seen giant spiders. They'd seen birds in the sky, and they heard the roar of animals they suspected were large and probably dangerous, but they hadn't seen any of them. Only rodents running around in the grass, and once a four-legged beast in the distance that didn't look very fast but was large.

When the sun set and it was dark, they retreated to the interior of the fish tank. Bakker, of course, was interested in the star fields and examined them closely through the glass top of the fish tank, but she found no recognizable patterns.

Hackett, standing next to her saw a dull red glow in the distance. He asked, "What's that?"

Bakker looked and said, "We saw no evidence of civilization, so I would guess it's not a city. Forest fire of some kind? A moon rise? Maybe a volcanic eruption. There are any number of things it could be."

Clark moved close to them and said, "I'd vote against a volcano. We didn't see any smoke or dust during the day. We would have seem something like that if it was a volcano."

"Could be that be the wind was blowing from the wrong direction, or you might have missed it completely," said Bakker.

"We can go look tomorrow," said Hackett. "Can't be that far away."

"Distances can be deceptive," said Clark. "It might be well out of our range."

"If it is, we don't have to worry about it," said Hackett, tired of the discussion already.

Cheney moved to the hatch and stepped out. She leaned back and called, "It's very nice out here. Cool. Pleasant."

Munyoz, who had been dozing in one of the chairs, opened her eyes and looked out at Cheney. With effort, she pushed herself up and walked to the hatch. She hesitated, as if afraid of something in the dark, and then ducked through.

Hackett looked at Bakker and said, "I think I'll go outside, too."

He crossed to the hatch and stepped out into a warm night with a light breeze. He thought he could smell smoke and wondered if what made the glow was a forest fire and not a volcanic eruption. He remembered a massive forest fire on Earth, somewhere near the West Coast that spread smoke over half the United States when he was much younger. He thought he could smell the smoke of that fire, though he had been literally thousands of miles from it.

The sky overhead was filled with stars, and there seemed to be a sameness to it. It looked like the night sky he was used to seeing, but it wasn't quite right. It was as if some of the stars had shifted their positions slightly so that the constellations were distorted. There were hints of Ursa Major and something that might have been Orion, but the stars in the belt had migrated, so that they no longer formed a nearly straight line and the four bright stars that had marked the perimeter of the constellation had been reduced to three in a lopsided triangle.

The moon had risen, and Hackett studied it. It was a half moon and there were hints of huge craters and several dark spots that looked like those on Earth's moon, but there wasn't really the "man in the moon." It reminded him of a model built by an unskilled adolescent. Familiar in a vague way but not quite right.

Bakker joined him and almost as if reading his thoughts, said, "The sky is slightly scrambled."

"Yes. Does that do anything for you?"

She shrugged and then aware that he wasn't looking at her, said, "Not without a lot of computer time."

"You going to identify it?"

"Meaning the sky?"

Now Hackett looked at her. "You know what I mean."

"Yes, I think I'll be able to identify the planet and the system."

"You sure?"

"There are some things I'll want to check, but I'm fairly sure that I can. The first time the sky was a mess and nothing recognizable in it. Now there are some things I do recognize, or think I do."

"Then we're making progress."

"Yeah," said Bakker, "but like I said, I fear that no one is going to be happy with my answer."

[3]

THE NIGHT HAD BEEN FILLED WITH ROARS, screams, cries, and the distant rustling of the grasses that sounded more like some low creature scrambling along the ground than the wind. The moon and the stars had lit the landscape so that the night was not black, but gray. Hackett was surprised about how well he could see until the moon set, but even then the land had not turned pitch black.

He went back into the fish tank, pushed some of the equipment around, and laid down. He listened as Munyoz and Cheney talked quietly outside and to the night sounds that might have come from a savannah on Earth before the human race had risen to dominance.

He woke up as the sun rose, the rays slanting down into his eyes. He sat up, saw Bakker slumped in a chair, asleep, and saw that Clark was standing near the hatch, looking down toward the river. The others were not in sight.

He climbed out of the hatch and said, "Quiet night."

Clark grinned broadly and said, "You were sleeping pretty soundly."

"Meaning?"

"Some interesting noises about two o'clock or so. Sounded like something had been caught in the open by a pride of lions. The roaring went on for the better part of an hour."

Hackett was disturbed that he could sleep through

something like that and then realized he had been in no danger. Maybe his subconscious had known that and let him sleep. The reflexes he had developed in the combat arena had come back to him without missing a beat. Had he been in some kind of danger, he would have awoken immediately.

"See anything?"

"Too dark, but it sounded like it came from down by the river. The lions caught something that needed to drink. I thought I might walk down there and have a look."

"If you didn't see them, how do you know they're lions?" asked Hackett.

"Well, I'm calling them that," said Clark. "But they can't actually be lions. What are the odds that lions would evolve on two distant planets?"

"Not great, I would imagine."

"I'll take one of the rifles with me. That should be sufficient, in case they're still there."

Hackett yawned and stretched, listening to the popping of his body and realizing he wasn't that young anymore.

"Mind if I tag along?"

Clark said, "Knock yourself out."

Hackett ducked back and grabbed a weapon. He held it up, checked it carefully, and made sure the safety was on. Then he exited the fish tank and joined Clark. Together they began the walk down the slope to the river.

They didn't see anything other than an early morning fog that hung near the bases of the trees and out onto the slow-moving surface of the river. There was a chill in the air, but it wasn't unpleasant.

And there was an odor of fresh copper. It was a smell that Hackett recognized as spilled blood.

Clark asked, "What's that smell?"

"Blood."

"That strong?"

"Means there's a lot of it."

They walked through the trees and were on the bank of the river. They noticed motion across from them, and Hackett saw some kind of four-legged beast over there. It seemed to be heavy, with short, stubby legs like a hippopotamus or maybe a rhino. The head looked more like that of a hippo. Hackett didn't remember if real lions attacked hippos or not, and he didn't think that they were dangerous to humans unless they were enraged. Besides, it was on the other side of the river.

Clark's attention was on something closer to him. He touched Hackett's shoulder and pointed. "There."

Hackett remembered that once lions ate their fill, they left. But other animals, scavengers, finished off the scraps. Those scavengers were often as dangerous as the lions. Of course that was on Earth, and there was no guarantee that the dominate predators and scavengers would behave in the same way on this new world.

They walked to the pile of bones splattered with red. There was skin pulled away and lying nearby, and still some meat, though not much.

"Well, they got something," said Clark, "whatever they are and whatever it was."

As they approached, Hackett saw something that didn't look natural. He bent down to examine it and then, in horror, called, "This looks like part of a shoe."

[4]

AT THE FISH TANK, HACKETT TRIED TO GET A head count. Bakker, Cheney, and Munyoz were missing. Just as he was about to call out to them, Bakker and Cheney appeared, walking over the top of the ridge.

"Where in the hell have you been?" demanded Hackett.

"What the hell business is it of yours?" Cheney shot right back.

Bakker laughed and said, "A little privacy was called for. You know?"

Hackett said, "Munyoz with you?"

"I haven't seen her," said Bakker.

"She went out last night," said Cheney. "I didn't see her this morning."

"Crap," said Hackett.

"What's going on?" asked Bakker.

"I don't know," said Hackett. "We're trying to get a count on everyone."

"Well, she wasn't back there with us," said Bakker. "We didn't see anyone in that direction. Maybe she's down by the river."

"That's what I'm afraid of," said Hackett.

Clark appeared and asked, "You find her?"

"No."

"What in the hell is going on?" asked Bakker.

"We found the remains of a kill this morning. Animals got something."

"Yeah? So?"

"There were bits of what looked to be a shoe."

Cheney turned white, reached out as if to steady herself, and then sat down hard. She didn't say anything.

"You don't think . . ." said Bakker.

"We don't think anything at the moment. We're beginning to looked into the possibilities. We're trying to get a complete head count."

"So what do we do?"

"Spread out and try to find Munyoz. Then gather back here and wait for retrieval."

In a few minutes they spread out from the fish tank, working their way carefully down the slope, looking for Munyoz, calling for her. The only response was the echo of their voices and the continued roaring from the beasts that remained hidden from them.

When they reached the riverbank, they worked their way through the trees, searching for some sign that Munyoz had been injured and was unable to call for help. They found almost nothing. Near a bush that was close to the water's edge, they found a bloodstained scrap of cloth. About twenty feet from that was another shoe, this one intact with a single small spot of blood on it.

Near that shoe were marks of a struggle that looked as if someone had attempted to escape into the river. Hackett knelt near the marks, studying them, but they told him almost nothing, other than that a struggle had taken place.

He could see where fingers had dug into the soft mud of the bank, as if trying to hold or to resist something. It was almost as if it was a silent scream for help.

"She make it into the river?" asked Bakker, her voice low and husky.

Hackett shook his head. "I don't think so. The predators caught her as she tried to get into the water. Dragged her back and then killed her over there, where the other part of a shoe and the bones are."

"They don't look human," said Bakker. She purposely kept her eyes on the shoe. She didn't want to see the bones or the bits of meat left by the predators.

"Most of them are crushed," said Hackett. "Besides, I think they caught something else. Two kills and one feeding site. Everything is mixed in together."

"Crap," said Bakker.

Hackett looked up at her. "You okay? You don't look so good."

"Must have been horrible." She wanted to say more but fell silent.

"Well, we didn't hear anything last night. Probably was fast," said Hackett.

"Still, she had to know."

"I suppose so."

"She didn't have a weapon," said Bakker, quietly. "Everything looks so peaceful you just don't think about it. You don't think about weapons."

Hackett stood up and surveyed the area. "But we heard the calls. The roars. We knew there could be something out here that was big and dangerous."

"You just don't think of getting eaten in the world today," said Bakker.

"We're not on our world," said Hackett.

"Mars has no big predators," argued Bakker. She was just talking to keep the horror out of her mind. "We just don't think in those terms anymore."

Hackett wanted to end the discussion. "I think we know what happened to Munyoz. We can head back to the fish tank."

"You're taking this very well," said Bakker angrily.

"What would you have me do?" asked Hackett. "There is nothing we can do now."

Bakker looked as him as if she was about to respond, but she said nothing.

CHAPTER 15

[1]

THOSE WHO HAD REMAINED IN THE CONTROL room, in the hangar, knew that something was wrong, but they weren't sure what it was. The link between them and the fish tank, which had been so strong and effective on the first manned expedition, was somewhat less than perfect this time. The individual readouts for the explorers were sporadic and often incomplete. The signal seemed to fade in and out, almost as if they were being broadcast over a long distance, which, of course, they were.

The technicians were, at first, concerned by the failure of the signals to remain constant and steady but they always came back, sometimes after a few minutes and sometimes after as much as an hour. Nothing they seemed to do improved the situation, so they stopped working on it.

When Munyoz's vital's faded, no one thought much of

it. There was a spike in heart rate and blood pressure, followed by a sudden drop in blood pressure, and then a complete loss of signal. The technicians, sitting comfortably in their control room, who were worrying about how cold it was getting or how tired they were, couldn't get overly concerned about a problem that seemed to be with the equipment. Instead, rather than alerting the team in the fish tank that they had lost the signal, they waited for it to come back.

It did not.

When it was dawn on the planet, some two hours after Munyoz's signal had been lost, they thought about calling O'Neill to tell him about the trouble. They thought about trying to alert those in the fish tank as well, but in the end, they did nothing at all.

O'Neill entered the control room early and asked for a status report.

"Everything is fine," said a technician.

"Anything unusual happen during the night?"

The technician began a rundown of the observations made through the fish tank. He illustrated the briefing with some of the pictures that had been sent back through the fish tank and made comments about them.

Then, almost as an afterthought, he said, "We lost the signal for Munyoz last night." He glanced up at one of the chronometers and added, "About five hours ago."

O'Neill felt a chill run down his spine, but he tried to keep his emotions under control. Quietly, he asked, "Any idea why?"

"Equipment malfunction is our guess. We've been experiencing some interference throughout the night."

"Anything from the fish tank?"

"We didn't ask, but they didn't say anything to us, so we assume equipment malfunction."

O'Neill didn't like the sound of that. Assumption created misunderstanding and mistakes. He said, "Find out for certain, right now."

The technician turned in his seat and then leaned into a microphone so that he could talk to those in the fish tank.

While the technician attempted to establish verbal communication, O'Neill was on his feet pacing around the control room. He knew pacing did no good, but it burned off his nervous energy, and at that moment, that was about the only thing he could do.

[2]

THE SEARCH OF THE AREA TURNED UP SOME scraps of cloth that they assumed had belonged to Munyoz. There was no evidence of a civilization, or of any intelligent life, so it had to have been hers. That only underscored the too-obvious conclusion. Munyoz had not survived the night.

Hackett, having seen enough and knowing that somehow Munyoz had fallen victim to one of the world's predators, walked slowly back up the hill. He looked back over his shoulder, only to see the others in among the trees, still looking for some proof that Munyoz was dead. He knew that there was no hope and no need to continue the search.

He reached the fish tank but didn't enter. Instead he turned and surveyed the landscape. Beyond the tree line, on the other side of the river was a large dark mass that hadn't been there the day before. Momentarily he was puzzled by it. Then he noticed that it was moving, flowing, slowly down the slope toward the river. It was a gigantic herd of animals moving as one.

The rest of the team finally left the trees and were climbing the hill, heads down, as if tired or sad. They all knew that Munyoz was dead.

As they approached, Clark asked, "You have anything here that you want to do?"

"Such as?" asked Hackett.

"Experiment? Exploration? Any assignment that hasn't been completed?"

"No."

"That's it then," said Clark. "We can go home. No need to stay here."

Hackett didn't like the decision. It felt almost like they were retreating in the face of the enemy. That was a ridiculous thought, of course, but that was what he thought.

Bakker said, "Nothing." She shuddered. "They ate her."

"Yeah, I guess they did."

"You sound pretty damned cavalier about it, Hackett," she snapped.

"What do you want from me? There is nothing I can do about it now. It's not like I haven't been in this kind of situation before."

"You mean with something eating teammates?" she asked angrily.

"No. Losing people in the field. You need to concentrate on the job at hand. You mourn the dead when you get out of the immediate situation."

"Crap," snapped Bakker. "Sometimes I don't think I know who you are."

Hackett shrugged. "Sometimes you don't."

Clark walked past them and entered the fish tank. He looked at the main screen and leaned toward it and began to speak.

Outside they could hear his voice but not the words.

Cheney moved closer to them. "What are we going to do?"

"Not much we can do," said Hackett.

Bakker shook her head and said, "That might not be completely true."

"What do you mean?" asked Cheney.

"Do you know where we are?" she asked.

"No. I thought that was your job," said Cheney.

"Yes, and if I'm right . . ."

"You mean you do know where we are?" asked Hackett.

"I have an idea, but I want to have a look at the star fields with the help of the computer. I will say this one thing. How many planets have a single satellite?"

"This is no time to get cryptic," said Hackett.

Bakker nodded but said, "We've explored two worlds, and both of them had a single satellite."

"Well," said Cheney, "we don't know that. We've only seen one on each of those worlds, but the orbital mechanics might have kept additional satellites hidden for the short time we were there."

"This is not the time or place for a scientific debate," said Hackett.

"Yes," agreed Bakker. "This is something we can take up a little later."

Hackett entered the fish tank. Clark was sitting in one of the seats staring out at the trees along the river. He looked up and said, "They're going to recall us as soon as we're all back in the fish tank."

Cheney, who had just entered asked, "Even without knowing where Munyoz is?"

"We know where she is," said Clark. "There is really no doubt about what happened to her."

Hackett dropped into one of the chairs and said, "I'll just be glad when this is over."

Bakker, who had followed him into the fish tank said, "It's not ever going to be over."

Hackett stared at her but didn't ask what she meant. He didn't want to know.

[3]

AS SOON AS THE FISH TANK HAD RETURNED TO the hangar, and as quickly as he could walk across the hangar floor, O'Neill was at the hatch. The lock spun automatically, and the door swung open.

Without stepping in, he shouted, "What in the hell happened?"

Hackett said, without waiting for Clark to speak, "Munyoz apparently wandered off in the night. We suspect that she was killed by animals on the new world."

"You suspect? You didn't make sure?"

Bakker stood up and said, "If you have a minute before we get into this, I might have a solution."

O'Neill, believing that the hatch had warmed sufficiently for him to touch the metal, put his hand on it and stepped into the fish tank.

"A solution? You mean she's not dead?"

Bakker looked at the others, hesitated, and repeated, "I think I might have a solution."

"Then why don't you give it to us now?"

"I want to check the star fields. That will provide confirmation," she said.

O'Neill waited for further explanation, but Bakker said nothing more. She picked up her personal gear, stepped around the others, and exited the hatch. O'Neill was startled by her and merely stepped aside as if agreeing to what she had said.

As she walked across the hangar floor, O'Neill asked, "Anyone have any idea what she's going to do?"

"No," said Clark.

O'Neill looked at Hackett and waited.

"I certainly don't know what she's thinking. Munyoz is dead. We found the remains of her clothes and parts of her shoes. The predators got to her."

O'Neill looked at the control room and then back into the fish tank. "You don't know what this is about?"

"No."

[4]

BAKKER ENTERED THE CONTROL ROOM, LOOKED for a familiar face among the technicians, but found none. One of them looked very young, so Bakker said to her, "I want everything you have on the star fields from last night. Up on the screens."

There was a moment's hesitation, and the technician turned to the control panel. She made a few adjustments, and the first of the fields appeared.

Bakker sat down, aware suddenly that she hadn't bathed in a couple of days and that the new world had been warm during the day. No one seemed to notice, so Bakker decided to ignore the problem.

To the technician, she said, "What's your name?"

"Rachel."

"Well, Rachel, I want you to project the movement of the stars, in that field, forward in time until they look like the night sky we see from here."

"Why?"

"Because I think it will work. Because I think it will help identify that planet we were on. But mostly because I said so."

"This might take a while," she said.

"Start with ten-thousand-year jumps, and if that doesn't progress us fast enough, then a hundred thousand. If that doesn't do anything, we'll bump it up to million-year jumps, but I think we might overshoot if we do that."

Rachel didn't understand the reasoning, but she turned back to the console. She worked at it for a moment and then said, "This is the sky ten thousand years from now."

The stars began jumping forward as they moved through the galaxy in relation to the Earth and Mars. It wasn't quite as fluid as Bakker had expected, but the transitions were fast enough that they were progressing rapidly through the eons with the sky changing.

Bakker leaned back and watched the screen as each of the fields progressed and the stars continued their dance. Slowly the sky changed from vaguely familiar patterns into the constellations that were seen every night in the sky above Mars. They looked like they always had to her.

"Stop," said Bakker. "How long?"

"What?"

"How many years have passed?"

"This is the field projected four million years into the future," Rachel said.

"No," said Bakker. "The field we started from is the sky four million years ago. I know where we were."

[5]

BAKKER STOOD IN AT THE HEAD OF THE TABLE. The rest of the team and O'Neill sat there. Behind her was the star field as they had seen it from the new world. She let it cycle through, rapidly until it was the field as they saw it every night. She let that sit there for a moment and then started the cycle over again, without commenting on it.

Clark finally asked, "What are we seeing here?"

"Don't any of you get it? I start with the stars as we saw them on the new world, and I end with the stars as we see them each night."

"I don't get it," said Langston.

Hackett shook his head in disbelief. "You're saying that we never left the Solar System."

"Somehow, we were projected from here to Earth."

"That wasn't Earth," said Clark. "Where were the cities? The people?"

Bakker looked at Hackett. "You want to tell them, Tom?"

Hackett felt cold. He felt frightened. The implications of what Bakker said were staggering. He wasn't sure that her methods were accurate, but he didn't know enough about her methods to refute what she was suggesting.

"Doctor Bakker is telling us that we have not traveled to a distant planet in our exploration. She is suggesting that we traveled back in time."

CHAPTER 16

[1]

O'NEILL, QUITE NATURALLY, DIDN'T WAIT LONG
to leave the briefing room. His mission was to carry the information he had to his superiors. It changed nearly everything, providing, of course, that Bakker was right.

He hurried down the corridor, turned, descended a short flight of stairs, and then headed out, through the main doors and onto a raised plaza. He crossed it quickly, descended another set of stairs, and was on the ground level in the middle of the Martian city. There were a few people on the street, which was more of a greenbelt than an old-fashioned paved road, despite the late morning hour.

O'Neill ignored them all, found the building he wanted, and entered. He used the long escalator that took him directly to the second floor. He found Sally Clinton's office and was delighted to see that William Curry was there, talking with her.

Without preamble, he announced, "I think we have some trouble with our project."

Curry turned in his chair so that he could face O'Neill. "What is it?"

"I don't think we're traveling through interstellar distances as we thought. I think we're moving through time. Traveling into the past."

Clinton snorted her disbelief. "Are you suggesting that you invented a time machine?"

O'Neill shrugged and said almost helplessly, "I don't know what I invented. We invented. All I can tell you is that the evidence now suggests the machine moves through time and not space, though it does seem to manifest itself on Earth rather than remaining on Mars. I don't know why that would be, but that seems to be the case."

Curry leaned his face on his hand and massaged his chin. "Time travel? What makes you think it's time travel?"

"I'll have a full report prepared later that will contain the evidence, including the observations of the team we sent out. But the real clues seem to be the star fields that we were going to use to identify the planets, and the single satellite circling the world. Both suggest time travel. We were looking at the sky as it was four million years ago."

"I can't accept this," said Clinton. "Time travel is not theoretically possible. The very paradoxes established by time travel make it impossible."

"I'm not prepared to argue advanced time travel theory," said O'Neill. "I'm only telling you what we believe to be the situation."

"Calibration," said Curry. "Have you been able to calibrate the fish tank?"

O'Neill looked at him as if he had lost his mind. Now the man wanted a *calibrated* time travel machine?

"No," he said simply.

Clinton waved aside the comments. She started to speak, stopped, started again, and then stopped again.

"Yeah," said O'Neill. "My mind was boggled, too."

"What do you plan to do?" asked Curry.

"I haven't thought about that in any sort of depth. Your comment about calibration seems to be the important one. If we can't control where the fish tank goes, then we've got an interesting toy but no real tool. With calibration there are endless possibilities."

"Who have you told about this?" asked Clinton.

"Just you two."

"And who else knows?"

"Well the team, of course," said O'Neill. "And probably some of the technicians Bakker worked with to identify the planet. Actually, I think she was trying to identify the era rather than the location."

"Where are they now?"

"The technicians are probably still at the hangar. The team is in the city."

"Then you had better find them and tell them all to keep this quiet. We don't need any of this leaking before we are prepared for it.

"The team won't talk. They know that the experiments are classified. The technicians can be kept at the hangar until we can sort this out," said O'Neill.

"Let's keep it that way then," said Clinton. "Until we know exactly what we have."

O'Neill hesitated and then nodded his agreement.

[2]

THE MEETING BROKE UP WITH THE YOUNGSTERS heading home for the evening. Hackett just sat there, watching the holographic display cycle through the illustrations that Bakker had created to explain the situation. He didn't seem inclined to move and made no attempt at conversation.

"Do you know what this means?" asked Bakker finally. "In the greater philosophical sense, I mean?"

Hackett was still trying to wrap his mind around the idea that they had traveled in time. He didn't think it possible, and had seen nothing to actually prove it. He believed, at that moment, Bakker's theory to be incorrect.

Bakker didn't wait for him to answer the question. She said, "We can fix everything that ever went wrong. We know where the mistakes were made, and we can repair them. No Dark Ages. No plagues. No genocide, and no world wars. We can save the archduke, and we can stop Hitler."

"I don't—"

And then she said the thing that she had been thinking about since the moment she had seen the bit of shoe and the bloodstained ground. "We can go back and get Munyoz."

"But she's dead."

"Now," said Bakker. "But she wasn't last week, and if

we can get back before she wandered off by herself, we can keep her from doing that. She can survive the trip."

"Wait," said Hackett, thinking fast and remembering things. "I read somewhere that you can't meet yourself. If you do there could be some catastrophic explosion or consequence."

"Science fiction theory," said Bakker.

"Isn't what you just said science fiction theory?"

"No."

"Why not?"

"Because we know that we can travel through time now. And there is no reason why meeting ourselves would cancel us out in a blinding flash of light."

She smiled and added, "I've read those same science fiction stories."

Hackett stared at her and waited for more.

"Okay," said Bakker, "I didn't want to get into advanced theoretical thinking here, but let's talk about this. The old classic is that you can't go back through time to kill your grandfather, because then you wouldn't exist and therefore couldn't go back. But, since you are the instrument of the change, you must exist, and therefore any change you made wouldn't cancel you. It might take out your siblings and your grandfather's children, but not you. Science fiction thinking for the plotting of a story, maybe, but with an element of logic to it."

Hackett looked down at the floor and thought about that for a moment. "Okay. I can see that. But how exactly could we meet ourselves?"

"We aren't really meeting ourselves, but meeting people who are a week or ten days younger then we are now. Think of it in terms of inanimate objects. I pick up a PDA and carry it back in time. I can set it next to the same PDA because the one I have is a week older."

"That seems to be talking in a circle," said Hackett. "At some point they need to rejoin."

"Well, maybe it's because, in this case, time is a circle and we are cutting across it to a different point. The real issue here is that meeting ourselves back then won't cancel out them or us. If we all traveled through time, then there would always be both of us. However, if we leave our earlier selves there, after making sure that Munyoz doesn't go for her fatal walk, then everything should melt back together on the timeline."

"You worked all this out in the last few hours?" asked Hackett.

"No. I was getting suspicious on the new world. I mean, there were clues in the night sky. The vegetation looked an awful lot like that of Earth and the animals we saw looked familiar. Then there was the moon. Looked like ours. The patterns on it were four million years younger, but I really didn't expect to see a single satellite around a planet that would look so much like ours."

"So when we learned that Munyoz had been killed," said Hackett, "you were already thinking about going back to rescue her before she got killed."

"Yeah. I'm not sure that it'll work, but to me, she wasn't lost as irretrievably as it seemed to the rest of you. It's just a question of making the trip."

To Bakker, the plan was foolproof. All they had to do was fine-tune the calibration, enter the new world a few hours before they originally arrived, and warn Munyoz when she showed up. It all seemed so simple.

[3]

As O'Neill left her office, Clinton turned toward the flat-screen on the wall. She glanced at Curry and said, "You going to stay for this?"

"Sure."

There was a moment while the connection was made, and when Bruce Pierce appeared, Clinton said, "I want full-security screen, no access except by Pierce, Clinton, and Curry. Accept?"

Pierce reached over and touched something and then said, "Accept."

When she saw that she had his attention, she said, "I think we have a new problem here."

Pierce hesitated, almost as if wondering if the communication channel was secure enough, but said only, "Tell me what you have, and I'll decide if we need to bother the others."

Clinton glanced at Curry and then back to the screen. "I'm a little reluctant to discuss this, but only because the idea is so far out in left field."

"We have trouble with our travel?"

"That's what I don't know. O'Neill was here a few minutes ago, and he says that we haven't beaten the interstellar travel problem."

Pierce interrupted. "What in the hell are you talking about?"

"We thought we were traveling interstellar distances with the fish tank. O'Neill said that he thinks we're traveling through time."

"Time travel is impossible," said Pierce.

"We said the same thing about faster-than-light travel, and interplanetary flight, but here we are."

"I don't need a lecture," snapped Pierce, "nor do I need a class on the scientific age of enlightenment. There are some things that simply are impossible."

He held up a hand to stop her response and added, "Or if it will make you feel better, impossible, given our state of technology."

"Which doesn't rule out time travel," said Clinton.

Pierce seemed to look beyond her and said, "Who's that behind you. Curry? You go along with this nonsense?"

Curry leaned forward, in toward the center of the frame, and said, "Well, I don't have a lot of information about this, but I have to agree with Sally here. Time travel does seem like an impossible feat, given what we know."

Pierce leaned back in his chair, tented his fingers under his chin, and fell silent. He made no move to disconnect. He stared down, as if lost in thought.

Finally he said, "I don't see how this changes anything at all. The basic mission can be accomplished whether we travel through space or time."

"Will you inform the others?"

"I'll have to," said Pierce. "But, we need to keep to the schedule. Either way, we've made some good progress here, and if you're right—"

"O'Neill is right," corrected Clinton. "O'Neill and Bakker are right."

"Yes, whatever. If they are right, then we have succeeded in our mission."

"Then we do nothing?"

"Just let the missions run and keep an eye on them. And let me know if this time-travel theory proves out."

"All right," said Clinton. "Like I said, I thought you should know."

"Thank you."

The picture disappeared, and the connection was broken. Clinton spun around in her chair and said, "He didn't seem all that upset by this."

"He's right. It really doesn't change the overall mission, and that's all that is important."

[4]

IT WAS A HECTIC FOUR DAYS, MADE MORE SO by the idea that the mission had to be mounted quickly. Somehow they thought of Munyoz's rescue as a perishable item. If they didn't get back there as quickly as they could, she would be lost forever. Of course, if they had time travel, time was no longer the problem for them, but they were caught up in conventional thinking.

The control room crew was working fourteen hours a day, and even the night crew was working long hours.

O'Neill began a new training program for the travelers. The things they learned before were reviewed quickly, and then they moved into the realm of theory about time travel. The briefings were long on theory but short on practicality. Everyone was guessing about the consequences of time travel.

Bakker spent her time trying to gauge the scientific opinion about time travel and found that few had ever thought about it with a sense of possibility. The best sources for her were in science fiction, where the authors allowed their imaginations to run wild, to create worlds in which there was an internal logic not based on any experimental evidence. It was as she had said to Hackett. Time travel was in the realm of science fiction.

One night, sitting in her apartment, she looked over at Hackett who was sleeping on the couch, the television rolling through the channels on a unending search, because he was lying on the remote.

She said, her voice loud, "Are you asleep?"

When there was no response, she asked again, louder. When he stirred, she said, "This isn't going to work."

Blinking rapidly, unsure of what time it was or how long he had been asleep, he asked, "What isn't going to work?"

"All this theorizing about time travel. No one knows anything about it. We could screw up human history by making some subtle change in the distant past. Isaac Asimov suggested that in a novel where they were making the minimum change necessary to create a positive effect at some future time. Wilson Tucker had travelers roaming through history to record and explore historical events but being careful not to interact too much with the people they met. There was a book about the Alamo where time travelers went back to win the battle and change history, but they had to keep moving around in time to prevent drastic changes in the future, and I'm not sure they ever got it right."

"There is a trend there," said Hackett, sleepily. "Change in the past equals repercussion in the future."

"Yeah, but it's not scientific theory. It's only science fiction stories. Before we start messing around in the past, we need to know what will happen."

"Well, we've made two trips, and there haven't been any changes."

"How do you know?" asked Bakker. "The changes would affect us."

"No they wouldn't. We'd be in the past, when the ripples we create affect the future. When we returned to our time, we'd know if there were changes."

"But we haven't looked," said Bakker.

"And since we haven't noticed, then any effects must dampen out or be inconsequential. Or there might be none at all."

"Unless we were so far back in time that anything we did wouldn't affect us so far in the future."

Hackett grinned. "That, too."

"So, as long as we're going so far back, it doesn't make any difference."

"And," said Hackett, "we don't know that anything we do would have a major ramification even if we aren't very far back."

"Which means we can go rescue Munyoz and then make a real study to find out if we're changing anything."

"Of course," said Hackett.

[5]

THEY ASSEMBLED IN THE HANGAR, NEAR THE fish tank, and though the mission to rescue Munyoz really only required a single traveler, they were all there ready to go. They knew the trip would be a short one. They would return to the new world, find the first landing point, and then leave a warning. If they ran into the first travelers, that was fine, too. They'd issue a verbal warning and let it go from there.

Clark leaned close to Langston, who was standing near him, and asked, "Why are we all going?"

"Because we can," she said.

"Why not one, and why not someone who wasn't with us on the first trip?"

Langston ignored the question, because it was one that had been asked in the briefings, and had been answered there. One group had experience in traveling, and it really made no difference if one went or a dozen. The energy requirements did not escalate significantly after a certain point was reached. These were the people who knew what they were doing, what they had done, were friends with Munyoz, and they all wanted to go.

Langston didn't respond to Clark, because there was no reason to.

Hackett moved forward and looked into the fish tank. There were plenty of weapons stacked inside. This time they had a very good idea of what danger they faced. The weapons they had would bring down anything.

O'Neill hurried across the hangar floor, looking like a low-ranking executive who had been given some trivial last minute instruction.

He stopped near them and said, "It isn't necessary for you all to go."

Langston said, "We've just had that discussion, and we're all going."

"Okay. But remember, this is not a reconnaissance, it's a rescue. Don't stay a moment longer than you must."

"I'd like to get some star fields," said Bakker. "For comparison purposes."

"Why? You know what they're going to look like. We're going back to the same time," said Clark.

Bakker shrugged.

"Okay," said O'Neill. "In and out on this one. Once you have returned, we'll figure out what our next move is going to be. Just in and out. And don't do anything that might mess up the flow of time."

Remembering an old television program, Hackett said, "You mean don't sneeze?"

O'Neill shot him a nasty look and said, "We're still running simulations, but there is no reason for us to tempt fate here. Be careful and be quick."

"We'll just warn Munyoz, and we'll get out."

Clark said, "We won't even tease ourselves about being in the same place."

"Say, I've got a question," said Cheney. "How is it that we have no memory of visiting ourselves. Shouldn't we remember this trip?"

"No, because we haven't gone yet," said Clark. "We have to travel back to create the memory but once we do, then we'll remember it."

Hackett laughed and said, "Circles in circles."

"If you've finished with this idle chatter," said O'Neill, "we can get going."

They entered the fish tank, prepared for anything.

CHAPTER 17

[1]

THE FISH TANK CAME TO REST ON THE GENTLE slope of a low hill, not far from a river. The grass around it was short, dull, dried, and brown. Of the few bushes and fewer trees that they could see, all had lost their leaves.

The sky above them was a gunmetal gray, and it looked like it would snow soon. There was a wind that blew, but it was a light, pleasant breeze, and neither the grass nor the bushes near them reacted to it.

"Missed," said Bakker.

"Meaning?" asked Clark.

"That we are not in the same time as our last trip. This is either late fall or early winter. Last time we were here, it was the bloom of summer."

"I don't think we were here at all," said Hackett. "We missed."

Bakker turned to look at him and asked, "What do you mean by that?"

"This isn't the same place. The river is wider, and there are no trees around it. The hill isn't quite as high, and the slope is gentler."

"And that means we can't wait a couple of days before we arrive," said Cheney, grinning at the sound of that. Wait for themselves to arrive.

"No, because it'll be months before the conditions will be the same as they were on that trip," said Hackett, "assuming that we have undershot rather than overshot the target. We don't even know that."

"Do we take time to look around?" asked Bakker. "Help us calibrate the machine."

"What sort of clue would be available to you?" asked Hackett, waving his hand.

She merely shrugged in response.

"If there was a civilization around," said Hackett, "then we might be able to date it that way. We pick up anything for carbon dating, and the margin of error is such that it does us no good at all."

"Not to mention," said Cheney, "we don't know the date of our first trip."

"What's that?" asked Langston, pointing.

Coming over the hill was a large creature that looked like a giant, hairy ant, though the body wasn't segmented, and it had no feelers. It looked left and right as it lumbered closer. It was followed by a herd of fifty to a hundred.

"That's nothing from the fossil record as I studied it," said Clark.

"No," agreed Cheney. "I've never seen anything like it."

"That doesn't mean anything," said Hackett. "There are

probably thousands of creatures that are not in the fossil record or have yet to be discovered."

As he said it, he realized that there probably wouldn't be much more discovered in the fossil record. Nearly everywhere on Earth had been explored and then cultivated or converted to human habitat. Fossil hunters, going out into the desert to search were a thing of the past.

"We need pictures," said Cheney.

Bakker picked up a camera and started to shoot through the glass of the fish tank. Then, afraid that the glass would distort the photographs, she stepped to the hatch.

Outside it was colder than she had expected. She shivered but ignored the cold. She wasn't going to be outside that long. She stepped around the corner of the fish tank for a clear shot and raised the camera.

As she did, one of the creatures lifted its head and trumpeted its displeasure. It seemed to focus its attention on Bakker and her camera. She didn't seem to notice.

Hackett picked up one of the rifles. It would fire a fifty-caliber bullet with enough force that the projectile could penetrate an inch of armor plate. Of course, the recoil would blacken his shoulder, and he hoped he wouldn't have to fire a second round.

As soon as he was out of the hatch, he hurried around the corner and raised the weapon. He wouldn't fire unless the creature came much closer.

The movement near the fish tank seemed to enrage it. It trumpeted again, shook its bulky, black head, and then lowered it. Hackett saw that the eyes were high on the skull, protected by a ridge of bone or flesh. That meant it could see as it charged with its head lowered.

Bakker kept snapping pictures, surveying the herd with

the view plate on the back of the camera. She wanted to capture as much of the grazing activity as she could. She was concentrating deeply and seemed unaware that one of them was about to attack.

The creature trumpeted once more and then charged, its six legs working together. It covered the ground rapidly, and it was clear that its target was Bakker.

Hackett aimed, sucked in a deep breath, let half out, just as he had learned on the rifle range so long ago, and squeezed the trigger. The sound of the weapon wasn't as loud as he expected. Nor was the recoil as violent as he thought it would be.

As he worked another round into the chamber, he saw the first bullet strike the creature above the right eye. There was a faint mist of blood, bone, and other tissue. He was surprised that the shot had not felled the beast.

It stopped and raised up, off the front two legs, as if taking a fighting position, shook its head, and then toppled to its side.

He had thought the sound of the shot would scatter the others, but they hardly moved. Maybe they were so large that they feared nothing around them. Or maybe they didn't understand the danger. They kept on grazing.

Bakker whirled and shouted, "What in the hell?"

"It was charging."

She looked bewildered, as if the words made no sense to her and then looked back, at the body of the creature. The blood drained from her face, and she looked as if she was going to pass out.

"Let's get out of here," said Hackett.

Without a word, Bakker turned and entered the fish tank. Hackett followed her.

"Let's initiate the recall," said Hackett. "We've missed our target."

[2]

O'NEILL STOOD IN THE CONTROL ROOM LOOK-ing at the display screens and asked, repeatedly, "How have we missed the mark so badly?"

One of the technicians finally asked, "Why do you keep saying that?"

"Because this is clearly not the same place or time where the fish tank landed before."

"We set everything according to the indications from the records. It should have gone to the same exact place in space and time."

O'Neill stared at the screen feeling slightly sick to his stomach. He believed they had found time travel. They could "fix" human history, but not if they couldn't control the trip. What would happen if they dropped the fish tank into the middle of a battle, or an active volcano, or into a hundred other natural disasters that the remote-controlled robots didn't see or predict. Time travel was going to become as useful to them as a battery would have been to the ancient Babylonians if they couldn't figure out a way to control it.

"What went wrong?"

"I don't know," said the technician. "Power fluctuation? Our movement through space? I don't know."

O'Neill found a chair and dropped into it. He kept his eyes on the screens, watching the reactions of those inside the fish tank. He watched as the strange creatures came over the hilltop and moved, slowly, fanning out as they grazed. He watched as Bakker took pictures and then as Hackett shot one of the creatures with the most powerful of the rifles they had taken with them. The whole episode confused him.

"What are those things?" he asked.

A female technician said, "Giant ants, except ants that size can't exist."

"They're not ants. They look like ants but they aren't ants. They seem to be some kind of herbivore. Probably warm-blooded with an internal skeleton," said O'Neill without really thinking about it. "I don't recognize them."

"I can find nothing in the library about them. Only six-legged creatures we've ever encountered were on Earth, and they're insects. Nothing of that size."

O'Neill could see that the conversation was about to descend into a discussion of extinct life forms from Earth. He didn't want to listen to that, nor did he want the attention of the technicians to be diverted into such a discussion.

"There's the recall request," said O'Neill. "Let's get them back."

"They haven't gathered any samples. They'll be coming back with nothing."

"We have the observations. Let's just get them back so that we can start again."

[3]

As soon as the fish tank returned, Bakker was out of the hatch, demanding to know what went wrong.

"Obviously," said O'Neill, "the instruments are not as finely calibrated as we'd like them."

"We have to go back," said Bakker.

"Why?"

"Because we didn't fulfill our mission," said Bakker. "We didn't recover Munyoz."

"I fear that Munyoz is lost to us," said O'Neill. "We can't use all our resources to recover her."

Bakker stared at him as if he had gone insane. "Why not? It's all part of trying to understand this system. You just said the equipment is not calibrated correctly. A return to that point will help us calibrate it."

"Yes, maybe," said O'Neill, "but I think travels back into our historical past would be more useful. We need to find dates so that we can correlate the ratio between our settings and the arrival at specific locations."

"Bull," said Bakker. "We need to be able to hit the same target two times. That will tell us a great deal."

[4]

O'NEILL STOOD IN FRONT OF THEM AND SAID, "You know, there really is no reason for you not to go out again. The whole trip, even with a stop in the new time, wouldn't take more than an hour at the most."

"But that gives us no time to assess the danger there," said Clark.

"It's not like we're throwing you into an unknown environment," countered O'Neill.

Hackett laughed out loud. "Of course you are. You have no idea what time we'll land in, and it could be a world in an ice age or in the middle of volcanic activity that is changing the planet from a livable world into a hell-like spot."

"So we send in a remote first and then people."

"What the hell do you need people for then?" asked Cheney.

"To get out and look around. To find something that will help us date the trip."

"I'm sorry," said Hackett, "but that makes no sense. You can get a robot to do everything that we can."

"But the robot, no matter how well programmed, no matter how sophisticated is still a robot. These missions are going to take the finesse that only humans can bring to them."

"You can control everything from right here," said Hackett. "You don't need a living body on the site."

"Are you afraid?" asked O'Neill in a mocking tone.

"Of what?"

"Setting down in the middle of an ice age or a massive volcanic eruption?"

"I'm merely suggesting that we have no need for such speed," said Hackett. "We can work through this slowly and logically rather than going off half-cocked."

O'Neill grew tired of the discussion. He turned toward Clark, almost as if cutting Hackett out of the conversation. He said, "We want to try something a little different. Something that should drop you into a world populated with humans. Give some information for calibration that we can use for the rescue mission."

Clark looked at the others and finally at Hackett. He said nothing.

Hackett said, "That could be extremely dangerous, if we haven't worked out all the details of time travel."

"We believe we'd have already seen them. We want to do this. Launch in an hour." O'Neill looked from face to face, trying to read their thoughts.

Cheney finally said, "I don't see any harm."

Bakker shrugged her agreement. "We can go after Munyoz whenever we want. We have all the time in the world."

"If the others have no objection," said Hackett, "then count me in as well."

O'Neill clapped his hands together. "We'll make the arrangements. Please be ready at fourteen hundred."

[5]

THE FISH TANK CAME TO REST IN A VALLEY THIS time. In one direction, the valley was steep, the walls made of rock and stone, with little vegetation.

Across from that was a more gentle, forested slope. The trees looked just like they belonged on Earth, and that surprised Hackett, though he couldn't have explained why.

From somewhere was the sound of cascading water. They thought they could see flashes of reflected sunlight from a small stream, hiding behind a curtain of trees and bushes.

There was the sound of life all around them. Not just birds, but other animals running through the trees, chattering at or chasing one another.

At the top of the ridge, something moved, visible only briefly before vanishing behind the rocks.

"Looks like we've found something," said Hackett.

"Yeah, but what?" asked Bakker.

"Let's go look," said Clark. "The least we can do is climb the ridge. That should give us a pretty good view of the surrounding country."

Clark spun the wheel to open the hatch and stepped through it first. He looked back and grinned. "Do I get to name this place since I'm the first out?"

Hackett caught a glimpse of something on the ridge above them. This time it was more than just a shadow.

"I think it's been named," he said.

CHAPTER 18

[1]

IN THE LATE TWENTIETH CENTURY IT WOULD
have been called a teleconference, and in the twenty-first
century it was a video conference, and on Mars now, it was
a holo conference. It looked as if all the participants were
in the same room when they were scattered all over the
planet's surface. The only real difference between the real
thing and the holograph was that for O'Neill, the conference attendees were smaller than normal and floating
about a foot above the floor.

Clinton and Curry were there, looking somewhat
washed out by the bright lights. Sitting near them were
Travis and Pierce. Only Davis was missing, and no one
knew where he was. They didn't care enough to use the
tracking system to find him. The meeting could go on
without him.

O'Neill stood and walked toward the hologram, almost as if he wanted to become part of it. He stopped short, seemed to be looking into the faces of all those present, and announced, "It's time travel now."

"Yes. We understand that," said Pierce. "We have been informed about that. But that really doesn't change our plans here."

O'Neill sat quietly for a moment. He was trying to digest all that he had been told in the last twenty-four hours. He now knew that the purpose of the mission was to move the human race out of the Solar System. Time travel didn't exactly accomplish that.

"We can't pump thousands of people into the past," said O'Neill.

"Why not?"

"Because the chance that they would inadvertently make a change that would alter our world is too great. There would be some sort of evidence for us to find, not to mention that it's possible that any colony we start, regardless of how long ago, would survive into the modern world. That certainly would have to alter our history."

Pierce held up a hand and said, "Not if we send them far enough back."

"We don't know that," said Travis, taking up on O'Neill's argument.

"Send them far enough into the past, and there would be no record of it," said Pierce.

"The purpose of the exercise," said Travis, as if the others didn't understand, "was not to eliminate population, but spread it out of the single basket of the Solar System. Sending people into the past does not actually accomplish that mission."

O'Neill squinted and scratched at the back of his head. "So what do we do?"

"There is no reason to continue to send the fish tank out until this problem is solved," said Pierce. "No reason to risk additional lives."

O'Neill looked startled by the statement and asked, "What do you mean solved?"

"Our goal was not to travel through time but to move out, among the stars. We have not accomplished that mission. We have been diverted," said Pierce again to make his original point.

Thinking fast, O'Neill said, "But we can protect the human race by hiding them in the various times. The are literally millions of years where we can send people. We'll maintain contact with them."

"To what purpose? In the end, they're on Earth. We are trying to move them out among the stars."

"I think you're splitting a fine hair here," said O'Neill. "We accomplish the same thing, which is to protect the human race, as I understand the mandate."

"No, we don't. And, we risk the reality that we know by sending thousands, millions into the past. Now, we have to stop and figure out what we can do to travel through inter-stellar space and forget this time-travel project."

O'Neill looked from one holographic figure to the next. They were staring at him. He didn't fully understand the problem, and he didn't understand why they were pressing him.

He wiped a hand through his hair and said, "I'll recall our team as quickly as I can."

[2]

IT HADN'T BEEN MUCH OF A STRUGGLE TO reach the top of the cliff. There had been a path worn down by the feet of various beasts over the decades. If Hackett hadn't know better, he would have believed that it had been chopped out of the rock and forest by human hands sometime in the past. It was well worn, but there really was no evidence that there had been an intelligent design behind it.

Following him closely were Clark, Bakker, and Cheney. Novotny had remained with the fish tank in case something happened there and they needed help, and to keep any large animals away from it.

Hackett reached the top of the rocky cliff and then turned, looking back down at the others. When they joined him, they all were climbing the last few feet of the grass-covered hill. Now they could begin the exploration of the area.

It took a moment for him to understand what he was seeing when he stepped up on the high ground. The ground dropped away into a broad valley that looked as if it opened out onto an inland sea or a gigantic lake. Maybe it was the ocean itself. Hackett couldn't tell for certain because he couldn't see across it.

The harbor was what caught his eye initially. A huge, crescent-shaped area that looked as if it had been adapted to sailing ships. There were several docked there, but the rigging looked odd, and the shape of the ships was not quite right.

Across the harbor was a city. Not a primitive city that would be associated with sailing ships but something slightly more modern with several high-rise buildings of fifteen or twenty stories. Not brick and stone structures either, but something of glass and steel that looked strange. The windows somehow didn't look right.

In fact the whole city was slightly off kilter. The streets were wide but not straight. They all curved, almost as if they were part of a gigantic circle. Hackett suddenly thought about Atlantis. Maybe they had found the lost city.

"I don't see any people," said Bakker.

"We're too far away to see individuals," said Hackett.

"I don't see any cars, or wagons. They must have them. The streets are wide."

Clark stared for a moment and then smiled, saying, "I think we've solved the mystery of Atlantis."

Hackett turned to him. "I thought that, too."

"But I don't see a volcano. Isn't there supposed to be a large volcano nearby?" asked Bakker. "One that erupts and wipes out the city?"

"Maybe it's dormant."

"Do we go down there?" asked Cheney.

"I don't see why not?" said Hackett. "Might give us a clue about the date."

"What if they're not friendly? What if they see us as enemies?"

"Why?"

"I don't know," said Clark. "It's just that we'd be four strangers walking into their city. We don't know anything about them. We can't speak the language."

"How do you know that we can't speak the language?" asked Cheney.

"What language did the Atlanteans speak?" asked Clark.

"Assuming that this is Atlantis," said Hackett. "We don't know that."

"What else could it be? There is nothing like that city in the recorded history of Earth. It has to be Atlantis. Or this isn't Earth."

"Look at that place," said Bakker, interrupting. "They have a seaport. They'll be used to strangers. We go down there, and we can answer the questions about what this place is."

"I do this under protest," said Clark, "It seems dangerous to me."

They started down the hill then, found another path, one that looked almost like a road. The surface had been scraped smooth, and there seemed to be a slight rise from the edges toward the center, just enough to cause rainwater to flow to the sides.

"Shows a little engineering," said Bakker.

"Strange combination of the primitive and the modern. Dirt road that has been engineered to avoid standing water, but it's still dirt, not gravel, or any sort of paving."

They walked on in silence. Hackett expected to see aircraft in the sky above them, except there had been sailing ships in the harbor with no sign of anything that used steam or diesel engines. There were high-rise buildings that suggested an advanced age, but no sign of the machine technology that went with it. The whole time period seemed to be a contradiction.

They passed a cultivated field where a strange plant grew. There was a partial rock wall, with a split rail fence protecting it. Across the field, two or three hundred yards away was a farmhouse, though it seemed to have been built low to the ground, almost as if a pit had been dug and then roofed over. They couldn't see much of it, other than the roof and a stone chimney.

"I've never seen anything like that," said Cheney, pointing at the crop.

"Some local vegetable," said Hackett, but he didn't believe it.

There seemed to be nothing edible on the plant. The leaves were thick and heavy, and the stem, or vine, thick and spiny.

They heard a distant roar but couldn't tell where it came from. For all they knew, it was some kind of machinery, though they'd still seen no signs of machines.

They climbed a shallow hill, reached the top, and once again found the city spread out in front of them. This time they were close enough to see some real detail. The closest buildings were shorter than those in the center. The doors had an odd, curved shape to them, and all the windows were oval.

Now they could see movement in the streets but could not tell anything about the people. The clothing seemed to have a greenish cast to it. In fact, the colors in the city ran toward earth tones.

They walked on, confident in their ability to communicate with the residents of the city and hopeful of finding some way of securing the date. The date would be the first step in calibrating the time-travel system.

A coach crested another of the short hills and came to an abrupt stop. The animals pulling it looked strange. They were shaggy beasts that resembled camels more than horses. But their hair was longer, there wasn't much of a hump on their backs and their heads were more horse-like than camel. None of the travelers had ever seen anything like them. No drawings, no pictures, and certainly no photographs.

The door of the coach opened and a figure stepped out onto the road. It was human in shape, meaning that it had two legs, two arms, and a human-sized head. But the color was wrong, the eyes large and catlike, and the hands had only three digits—a thumb and two fingers.

It looked reptilian.

"What in the hell?" asked Clark.

The creature seemed as surprised as the humans. It lifted a hand as if to point and let out a high-pitched squeal. The volume increased as if it expected to be heard, though there were no other creatures near it.

"Maybe we should retreat," suggested Bakker, taking a step backward.

Hackett glanced to the right, at a distant farmhouse and saw the door opening. Something appeared in the doorway, climbing upward, as if out of a pit. It was barely visible in the half light created by the trees. Hackett thought it was another of the reptiles, but he wasn't sure.

"Yeah, before they cut us off from the fish tank," agreed Hackett.

Cheney asked, "Where in the hell are we?"

"I don't know," said Bakker, "but I don't think we're still on Earth."

So Bakker had been wrong.

[3]

THEY DIDN'T ACTUALLY RUN BACK TO THE FISH tank, but they moved quickly. Without realizing what they were doing, they fell into a military formation with Clark on the point, Bakker and Cheney as the main body fifteen yards behind him, and Hackett as trail, about fifteen yards farther back.

Hackett kept an eye over his shoulder, looking for any sign of pursuit, though he didn't really expect one. Humans, confronted with alien humans, seen in the distance, with no reason to suspect they were alien, would probably react much in the same way as these creatures. In other words, they wouldn't give chase, because they would be confused by the encounter.

They reached the top of the ridge, near the valley where the fish tank was hidden, and looked down. There were other creatures near the tank, crowding close to one side of it. Novotny was inside, watching them, but making no move to get out or to do anything.

Clark, at the top of the ridge, dropped to one knee and watched in fascination.

Hackett, not wanting to be silhouetted against the skyline, walked over the top of the ridge and down it several feet before he crouched. Anything in the valley, looking up, might be able to see him, but it would be against a dark background of dirt and not the bright background of the sky. He wasn't calling attention to himself.

"What do we do?" asked Clark.

"For the moment, just watch them," said Hackett. "They don't seem to be hostile."

The creatures below seemed to be watching Novotny, unaware that there were more strangers in the area. They stood back, forty or fifty yards, studying the movements inside the fish tank. There were only three of them. Of course, no one knew how strong they were or how dangerous they might be. It might be possible to just walk up, open the hatch, and climb into the fish tank without any response from them.

"I think we need to get off this ridge," said Hackett. He took his pistol from under his shirt and checked it. That was reflex from military training.

Clark looked at him for a moment, and it seemed he was about to say something, but then didn't.

Without another word, Hackett started down the path toward the fish tank. He slipped on the gravel once, caught his balance, and continued on down.

The sound alerted the creatures. They all looked up at him, but didn't move toward him. Instead, they retreated, moving back, away from the fish tank, deeper into the forest, nearly out of sight.

As the creatures moved, Novotny hopped over some of the equipment and began spinning the wheel on the hatch. He threw it open and stepped out holding a rifle.

Hackett waved an arm and then shouted, "Let's go."

The others moved then, following him down the path, scrambling along it.

The creatures seemed surprised by the sound of the human voices. One or two of them moved forward, as if to get a better look, but there was no sound from any of them. They were simply spectators.

Hackett joined Novotny near the hatch and then turned to watch the others. Clark slipped, fell to one knee, but popped up again. He caught up with the others.

As they reached the fish tank, they ducked and entered. Bakker moved across to where the weapons were arranged and grabbed one. Then, unsure what to do, she stood where she was as if she was going to guard the hatch.

When the others were inside and buckling themselves into their chairs, Novotny ducked through the hatch, then waited for Hackett.

But Hackett stood there watching the creatures. They didn't seem to talk to one another but did seem to be communicating. One had its hand raised and was wiggling its fingers in some sort of a sign language, all the time grunting quietly as if adding to the communication.

The others looked on, reading the message but paying little or no attention to Hackett and the other humans. The creatures didn't seem to recognize the humans as threats, maybe not even as intelligent, but seemed to be curious about them.

Finally Hackett ducked through the hatch and Novotny closed it, spinning the wheel.

Almost at the same time he dropped into one of the chairs, the fish tank seemed to spin out of control, the scene outside disappearing in a white mist. Hackett had the thought that the creatures were going to be surprised by their disappearance, and then suddenly, the fish tank was back in the hangar.

[4]

BAKKER WAS IN THE CONTROL ROOM WITH O'Neill and Hackett, watching the video that had been collected during the trip. Hackett was listening to the discussion that Bakker was having with O'Neill, which he found interesting.

"This clearly isn't Earth in the past," she said pointing to a picture of one of the creatures.

"How do you know?"

"There is no record of a civilization that involved some sort of intelligent lizards."

"You don't know they were lizards," said O'Neill. "You don't know anything about them."

Bakker shrugged, conceding the point. "But they weren't human, either."

"So what are you saying?" asked O'Neill.

"That we weren't time-traveling. There is something else going on here. We ran into a strange civilization that was clearly on another planet."

"You don't know that either," said O'Neill. "You don't know what any of it means."

"I think we can rule out time travel. This was clearly somewhere else."

"Like where?" He pointed at the screen and asked, simply, "How do you know that we're not seeing a lost civilization that existed four million years ago? You yourself dated the star fields to four million years. And it could be some time even older than that. You don't know."

"I know that there is no record, anywhere, of a civilization that existed four million years ago."

"There have been anomalous objects pulled out of stone, out of coal that suggest civilizations that existed long before the human race began its climb to dominance," said O'Neill.

Bakker actually laughed. "Those are old wives tales. They have no basis in reality."

O'Neill took on a hurt expression. "They are not. I've read about them. They're called Out of Place Artifacts. OOPARTs."

"Well, if they have a name, it must be true," said

Bakker, sarcastically. "Certainly only things based in reality have names. Like the centaurs."

Hackett remembered having read something about OOPARTs. He joined the conversation.

"Seems to me that there was a story about iron nails being found in a block of granite. I read a couple of things about that," he said.

"Yes, but random anomalies aren't the same as evidence for a reptilian civilization that disappeared millions of years ago," said Bakker.

"What would you expect?" asked O'Neill. "Some civilizations that crumbled were only gone for a few hundred or few thousand years, and there wasn't much left of some of them for us to find."

"Yes, but there was always something found."

"Not of Atlantis," said O'Neill. He held up a hand to stop the response. "Yes, it might be a myth, but we have a story handed down through the ages of this complex civilization, and there is little, if any physical evidence of its existence. In fact, you might have just found it."

"Ignoring that for a moment," said Bakker, "what about the creatures? Surely you'd admit there is nothing in the fossil record to account for them."

"How complete is our knowledge based on the fossil record?" asked O'Neill. "We're still finding new dinosaurs, and we're still finding other fossils of creatures that existed even before the dinosaurs. Or, at least we were."

"Point taken," said Bakker, tiring of the conversation. "But I still say that there is absolutely nothing at all to support your idea, other than your random artifacts that probably have alternative explanations that are as viable."

"Okay," said O'Neill. "Then what's your explanation? If we're not traveling interstellar distances and we're not traveling in time, what else could it be?"

"That," said Bakker, "is the question."

CHAPTER 19

[1]

BAKKER SAT ON THE COUCH IN THEIR APART-ment, her head in her hands, and said, again, "I don't know. I just don't know what the answer could be."

"But you have some kind of idea, don't you?" said Hackett. "You have some kind of theory."

She looked at him and said, "There aren't endless possibilities. We thought it was interstellar flight, but we were wrong . . ."

"Because of the DNA," said Hackett.

"Earth-based DNA, traceable in our world. Even if DNA was the method of transmitting the genetic code on another planet, it wouldn't fall into earth-based combinations. It would be different. Therefore, the DNA we have collected on the trips proves that we never left our own Solar System."

"So that leaves time travel," said Hackett.

"Yet, what we just saw is not suggestive of time travel. It was not the Earth in the far distant past. There is nothing to indicate that."

"Maybe the future then," said Hackett.

Bakker shot him a glance, looking suddenly pleased and then, just as suddenly, frowned.

"No, I don't think so. The reptiles didn't have the technology you would expect in the future. And besides, they would have time travel so they would be around here, watching us."

"I'm not sure what that means," said Hackett.

"It means that a time-traveling race would be around, maybe manipulating things in the past. We'd have some indication that they could do it, and we'd know, meaning us here and now, because we can do it. No, I don't think that these creatures are from the future for a number of reasons."

"Not to mention they didn't look human, either."

Bakker wasn't satisfied, though. She said, "I would think that technology would survive in some form. Yeah, some inventions have been lost, but we've always known, in one fashion or another they were out there."

"Meaning?"

"I would think that something so far into the future that another intelligent species evolved would be able to build on our technology. Would build on the legacy that we left them."

"Even in the event of a catastrophe that wipes out our civilization?"

Bakker was quiet for a moment. "We know that some civilizations vanished, yet we do know about them. Their technologies did survive them, but have been outstripped by everything we've done. So, I think the technology would survive, especially with all the written records we've produced . . . or video records, or other types of records."

She stood up. "No. I think that if we were far into the future, then we would have seen a civilization that had built on what we started. Not on something that had retreated into the past with sailing ships and horse-drawn carriages. It would be a more technically oriented civilization than the one we saw."

"Even if it was another species?"

"Technology is technology. I'd say yes."

Hackett wasn't sure that he bought the argument, but it was little more than an academic debate. They really didn't know if the technology would survive the civilization or that those creating a new civilization would be able to recognize the old. It was all guesswork based on not much observation. They really knew very little about what they had seen.

"So," said Hackett. "We're left with an anomaly that is probably best described as interstellar travel of some kind and not time travel."

Bakker looked embarrassed. "I think I was a little too quick to embrace that. When you think about it logically, given all that we know, travel into the past really is impossible."

"So we're traveling to other stars."

"That would seem to be the logical conclusion, based on what we know."

"Even with the DNA problem?"

"Let's just say that a better theory is that we somehow

contaminated the samples and got a false positive reading. More and better sampling should eliminate that problem."

Hackett clasped his hands together and said, "Then we're really traveling to the stars?"

"That seems to be the best explanation." But she wasn't sure about that either. It didn't explain the star fields.

[2]

"THERE IS ONLY ONE REAL SOLUTION HERE," said O'Neill, sitting with Clinton and Curry. "We have to try to hit the same target again and gather more data."

"To what end?" asked Clinton.

"Well, first, to see if we can hit that target again. We've only tried that once, and we missed, but we don't know how badly we missed. We've made three trips that provided us with specific information. Returning to one of those locations would, naturally, give us more. Give us a much better picture of what we're doing and where we're going."

"Let me see if I understand this," said Clinton, a little sharply. "You originally thought we were traveling through space, after a fashion, and were arriving at planets in other stellar systems."

"Yes."

"Then, given the pictures of the star fields and some of the collected evidence, you thought we were actually traveling through time."

"Yes."

"And now you think that we're traveling through space again."

"Yes."

"Maybe we're actually traveling through time and space," said Curry.

"No. We were attempting to account for all the evidence. We think that contamination of the samples is more likely than time travel."

"So you want to try to return to a precise location?" asked Clinton.

"Yes."

"But you already tried that and failed. You wanted to return in time and stop Munyoz before she went down to the river and was killed by the predators."

"We didn't match the settings precisely," said O'Neill. "We knew that we had to go a little farther into the past, so we changed the settings slightly in an attempt to compensate for our movement forward in time and our desire to go a little bit farther back. That didn't put us in the same place. So, no, we haven't done that. Haven't really tried that."

Clinton took a deep breath, looked at Curry almost as if attempting to draw strength from him, and asked, "Are your . . . travelers, willing to make another trip?"

"They have no objections."

Clinton stood up, preparing to leave. "Fine. Then let's get some answers."

[3]

BAKKER STOOD IN THE CONTROL ROOM, WATCHing the technicians as they adjusted the equipment. She said, "We need everything to match exactly so that we end up in the same place."

One of the technicians looked at her. She said, "I've got it. I understand it. I don't need you standing there telling me how to do my job."

Bakker looked at the technician angrily and wanted to respond. But the tech was right, even if she wasn't polite. Bakker stepped back, out of the way, and watched as the tech finished her work.

"Okay," said the tech, "everything in here matches everything that we did for the second trip. You should land in exactly the same place."

Bakker was going to say that they didn't want the same place, but she was thinking in terms of time travel. The same place was fine because they would be there a week or more later. The same place was what they wanted.

"Thank you," said Bakker.

She left the control room and walked across the hangar floor to the fish tank. The others, Clark, Cheney, Novotny, and Hackett were there, waiting for her. Stepkowski was missing because he had gotten sick. Langston had opted not to go on the trip but gave no reason for her refusal.

Bakker climbed through the hatch and said, "We're all set. We should get back to the second world we explored."

"Should?" asked Hackett.

"Everything is set the same as it was for that trip. I don't know why we wouldn't hit it."

"Except that we're several weeks into the future from where we were," said Clark. "Did you compensate for that?"

"How? We don't know what effect it might have. If I was to guess, I would say that we'd arrive at the same spot but a couple of weeks into the future there. We'd find evidence of our last visit maybe, but we wouldn't return to the same temporal arena."

"Enough theory," said Hackett. "Let's just get this show on the road. Let's see what happens."

Clark glanced at the control room and held up a thumb, telling them to begin the journey.

Hackett thought, by this point, he would be used to the disorientation. He felt slightly sick, but it wasn't as bad as it had been during the first trip. He closed his eyes, wished that he hadn't, and when he opened them, the trip was over.

They were sitting on a flat plain that stretched nearly to the horizon. There were a few animals running about, but nothing he recognized easily because they were so far away. It looked as if they had landed in another deserted area.

And then he turned to look over his shoulder.

[4]

CLARK WAS THE FIRST TO SPEAK. HE ASKED, simply, "Are we back to time travel?"

Bakker studied the scene in front of them and said, "I don't think so. We're certainly not in the past."

"Then we're in the future," said Clark.

"And," said Hackett, "if that is right, we won't be able to get back."

"Will you two shut up for a moment and let me think?" snapped Bakker.

Hackett stood up and turned to look at what he thought of as a modern city. It was a mixture of the old and the new, the stone and brick and the glass and steel. There were short buildings and skyscrapers. It might have been New York or Chicago or even Denver, though he saw nothing to suggest mountains, which would rule out Denver.

"A human city?" asked Hackett.

"I should hope," said Clark.

Bakker said, "We need to identify this place. We need some more information."

"We could just take pictures," said Cheney, speaking for the first time. "Take pictures and get out before we make contact with the natives, whoever or whatever they are."

"That looks like an Earth city to me," said Hackett. "An awful lot like one."

"Which means we're on Earth," said Clark, "Except I don't recognize that city specifically. And I've studied the database."

"There are hundreds of big cities on Earth, and I wouldn't recognize many of them from the limited view we have from here. We'll need to go check if we want to know exactly where we are now."

Hackett grinned weakly. "Last time we did that we ran into, what, reptilian humanoids?"

"There really isn't much that we can do from here," said Clark.

"Not enough to just get pictures from here?" asked Hackett.

"It doesn't tell us much," said Bakker. "We need to take a closer look."

Hackett shrugged his agreement.

[5]

THIS TIME THEY APPROACHED THE CITY CARE-
fully, using the available cover to advance while trying not
to look as if they were using the cover. They wanted to be
able to spot the people before anyone spotted them.

There was a pathway through a wooded area that
looked like the remnants of a railroad right-of-way that
had been converted to either a hiking trail or a bike path. It
had all the elements of a similar structure on the Earth, except that it seemed to be exceptionally clean. No debris
like candy wrappers or soda cans, or rubbish from a dozen
other sources. The grass along the trail was neatly
trimmed, and the undergrowth, what there was of it, was
not too dense.

They listened for noise from others on the path, figured
that anyone would be talking so that they would be heard
before they were seen. That would give Hackett and his
team time to take cover so that they could observe rather
than be observed.

They walked for about an hour, listening to the birds
that sounded remarkably like those on Earth, hearing the
buzzing of insects that also sounded like those on Earth,
and in the distance, the sound of traffic that, again, resembled Earth traffic. They hadn't seen or heard any aircraft,
but that could be a result of where they were.

The path finally ended, and they found themselves at
the edge of the city. There were cars on the streets, buses,
trucks, and people. Humans. It looked just like an Earth
city, and yet there was something about it that wasn't quite
right.

Hackett dropped to a knee, almost like the lead soldier

on a patrol. He surveyed the territory in front of him, looking for something that was out of place. He had a feeling that something was wrong, but he wasn't sure what it was.

"It looks just like Earth," said Clark, his voice quiet, as if he expected trouble.

"Yes, just like it," agreed Hackett.

A strange vehicle appeared, hovering two or three feet off the ground, looking like the rest of the traffic. The lines of it were odd, somehow asymmetrical and the doors looked overly large and out of place.

"What in the hell is that?" asked Clark.

A moment later it touched down near the curb, and two humans, one male and one female, ran to open the door.

Another being, this one definitely not human, unfolded itself and stood up. It looked, more or less, like the creatures that had been seen skirting the edge of the Solar System, that had been the reason for the formation of the Galaxy Exploration Team so many years earlier.

And worse yet, it seemed to be in control.

CHAPTER 20

[1]

"WE HAVE TO GET OUT OF HERE," SAID CLARK.
"We have to get back to the fish tank."

"No," said Hackett. "Not until we get a few answers. I want to know what is going on. We have to know what is going on."

Bakker had slipped back, a little deeper into the vegetation, but kept her eyes on the scene in front of them. She said, "It doesn't look like they are hostile."

"No, it looks like they are in charge."

"What's that mean?" asked Clark.

"I don't have any idea what any of this means. Do you, Sarah?" said Hackett.

She wiped a hand over her face and thought rapidly. "This looks like Earth. There are people. Humans. But there are aliens, too. Extraterrestrials. It's almost as if the aliens we spotted so long ago came to Earth rather than by-passing us. Came to Earth and took over."

"We don't even know that this is Earth," said Clark.

Hackett looked at him as if he had gone insane and then pointed to the right. "Read the sign."

Clark started to do that and then realized the significance of it. He could read it. The sign was in English.

"We're on Earth," said Hackett.

"We're human," said Clark. "We speak the language then. We can mix with the population and learn what has happened here. Should be very easy."

"Nope," said Hackett. "Sarah and I went to Earth on a trip and ran into roadblocks every step of the way. Bureaucracy and computers blocked our paths. I'll bet this society is even more rigid than the free one on Earth . . . or rather on the Earth we know. We'd be spotted right away, and then we'd have trouble getting out of that trouble."

"Besides," said Bakker, "we don't know the customs. We wouldn't know how to act if one of the aliens confronts us. We don't even know how to act if one of the humans confronts us. Everything will have changed."

Clark studied the scene in front of him. The street looked like the concrete or asphalt streets he had seen in pictures of Earth. The buildings followed the architectural style of Earth, meaning that in a large, old city there was a mixture of types. Tall skyscrapers built in the 1930s, glass and steel of the late twentieth century, and the more pleasing, graceful structures of the twenty-second.

And while some of it looked just like the architecture on Earth, some of it had a strange quality to it. Maybe it was just the evolution of materials, building ability, and style that created the odd look.

The streets were lined with shops, and there were people on foot, walking around, as they always had. Some looked purposeful, heading to work or to meetings, while others strolled, looking in windows, watching the crowds. Life seemed to go on as it always had.

Bakker moved closer to Hackett and said, "There is one way that we can be sure that this is Earth."

"How?"

"Wait until night and look up at the night sky. If the moon is there, then we know. If the constellations match what we're used to seeing, then we know."

"Didn't we try that already?" asked Hackett.

"Yeah, but this time I know what I need to see. I know what to look for."

"And there is no need to go into the city?"

Bakker looked back out into the edge of the city and said, "I wouldn't think so. We can get all the information we need after the sun sets."

"Then all we need to do is head back to the fish tank, wait for night, and we'll have the answer."

"I think so."

[2]

WITHOUT A WORD, AND WITHOUT MUCH IN THE way of an order, they slipped away from the edge of the city, moving deeper into the trees until they found the path again. Now, they walked along the edge of it where they could retreat deeper into the trees if they felt it necessary. If someone was coming from the other direction, they would just fade into the trees until the person, or the alien passed. The rate of march, and the spacing between them took on the aspects of a military formation deep in enemy territory.

But they saw no one.

And nothing came close to them.

Neither the alien creatures who now seemed to run the Earth, nor the local human population were using the trail. It might have been abandoned in the recent past because there were some signs of wear.

The air above them remained clear of aircraft, there were no motor vehicles around them and no one with barking dogs searching for them in the trees. It was obvious that no one was searching for them or even knew that they had arrived. If they *had* been detected as they approached the city, apparently neither the human population nor the alien creatures were concerned about it.

Once, they thought they heard someone on the path in front of them, and they scattered into the trees, finding places to hide. Hackett dropped to a knee near the trunk of a thick tree that had a bush growing to its right. He could see the path through the leaves but knew that if he didn't move, no one on the path would see him. In the forest, it was movement that gave away positions. Those things that didn't move were rarely spotted.

But nothing appeared on the trail, and after fifteen minutes, it was clear that what they had heard was probably an animal of some kind. Hackett broke cover, stepped onto the path, and in minutes was joined by the others. They continued the journey back to the fish tank.

When they arrived, they saw that nothing had changed there. Given the position of the sun, low, near the horizon, it seemed that twilight couldn't be all that far off. All they had to do was wait for night and look up at the sky.

[3]

THEY HAD BELIEVED BECAUSE THEY HAD GOT-ten away from the city cleanly, and because they didn't think anyone had seen them, that once they had arrived back at the fish tank, they would be safe. They walked down to the fish tank, looked inside it. None of them felt like entering it. It was, after all, indoors, and at the moment, they all wanted to remain outside.

Hackett dropped to the ground, sitting on what looked like someone's front lawn. The grass was thick, short, and looked as if it had been mowed. It didn't look wild at all.

In fact, looking around carefully, he decided that they were in some kind of a park. One that had lawns and trees that had been purposefully spaced to allow some sunlight through to nourish the grass, while at the same time, providing shade. A park suggested people would be close, yet he had seen or heard nothing.

Then, suddenly, overhead, an aircraft appeared. It did not look like an airplane or a helicopter. It was more oval shaped, not unlike the flying saucers of myth. There was no aerodynamic reason for it to remain in the sky. It wasn't flying fast enough to create any lift, if the shape allowed for that. It remained aloft for some other reason, and to Hackett, that meant it was alien.

Clark pointed upward and said, "I think we've been spotted."

Hackett climbed to his feet, his eyes on the craft above

them. He ducked down, entered the fish tank, and still watching the oval, picked up a rifle. He had the impression that the oval was spinning, but there were no visible clues to give him the final answer.

"It's coming down," said Bakker. Her voice was high and tight, and a little shaky.

"General?" said Clark. It was the first time that he had referred to Hackett by his rank. It was also a question.

"Let's get everyone inside. Then we'll see what happens next."

"Yes, sir," said Clark without realizing that he had said it.

Hackett checked his weapon, found it loaded, and then chambered a round. He was a little surprised that he was using an old-fashioned, chemical reaction weapon, but then, he didn't have to worry about a high-tech malfunction. Sometimes the oldest, and simplest, was the best.

He stepped through the hatch so that he was back outside, standing on the grass, looking up toward the oval that was now hovering between him and the sun. That made it difficult to see, with sunlight streaming around it.

Then it slowly settled to the ground. Hackett had expected legs to sprout from under it, but that didn't happen. It just settled on the grass about a hundred yards away. Nothing changed for a few moments, and then, without a sound, a door, or hatch, opened and a ramp seemed to unfold itself, providing a way for the crew to get out.

"Here they come," yelled Hackett, back over his shoulder. He kept his weapon pointed up at the sky, ready to open fire if necessary.

Clark joined him, holding another of the rifles.

"You know how to use that?" asked Hackett.

"I've had a familiarization course with it and have fired at targets."

Hackett wondered how the gravity, lighter atmosphere, and the environment on Mars would affect marksmanship. He'd never fired a weapon on Mars and suddenly, momentarily, thought it would be an interesting experience.

"Don't fire unless I do. Aim for the torso and try to put two rounds into the target, if you find it necessary to shoot."

"Yes, sir." And then he added, "You know, we can initiate recall at any moment. We could be out of here before they get out of that ship."

Without answers to a couple of questions.

There was movement on the ramp, and something tall, slender, and nonhuman looking appeared.

Hackett touched the safety and snapped it off. He lowered the muzzle but didn't aim it at the creature.

Immediately behind it were two humans. One of them wearing a uniform of some kind. He raised his voice and said, "Lower your weapon and put it on the ground."

"General?" said Clark.

"Move back into the fish tank," said Hackett. "Wait for me there."

As soon as he began to move, the humans ran around the creature. One of them yelling, "You are not to go anywhere. Stay where you are."

Hackett didn't want to shoot, because he didn't know the situation.

"Get us ready to get out of here," said Hackett.

Clark lowered his weapon, turned, and jumped through the hatch.

One of the humans stopped and raised a weapon. Hackett remembered the old rules of engagement that he had lived by while in a war zone. You didn't assume hostility because someone else was armed. You did when they pointed weapons at you.

Hackett fired twice. The human with the weapon dropped as if his bones had suddenly melted.

The alien creature turned slightly and looked down at the body of the human. It made some sort of noise that sounded almost like a cry of anguish. He raised a hand, which looked like a catcher's mitt with snakes attached, but it stopped moving.

Hackett took a long look at it, because it was the closest he had ever been to an alien. He had seen pictures, as they had been modified so long ago, and he had seen one in the distance, as they watched the city. Now he was seeing one much closer and thought that it didn't look threatening. Just different. Slightly smaller than he would have thought. Uglier, too. But then it was an alien creature.

"General?" said Clark from the open hatch.

Hackett tore his eyes away from the alien and turned. "Let's go," he said.

[4]

THEY WERE ACTUALLY ABLE TO SEND THE FISH tank back to the same place. They had the settings, matched them exactly, and used a robot for remote viewing.

Hackett had worried that the aliens would be swarming all over the point where the fish tank had appeared in their world, but that wasn't the case. There was no evidence of anyone being there, now that it was several hours later. Maybe they had some kind of electronic surveillance, but he wasn't concerned with that.

The fish tank appeared in a dark world. Lights from it illuminated the terrain so that they could verify the location, and once that was done, the lights went out. The remote cameras began their surveillance of the sky. It wasn't long until the moon rose. By that point the question of the planet had already been answered. The constellations were all recognizable, Venus was hugging the horizon, and Jupiter was high overhead. When the moon rose, the familiar patterns on the face ended all debate.

Bakker stared at the moon for a long time, almost as if she had never seen it before. It wasn't as if the moon had been altered in some way. It was as familiar as it had always been. Though, having lived on Mars for a long time, she had gotten used to the two small, misshapen objects that rocketed through the heavens during the Martian night.

"This is Earth," she said.

"Even with the aliens?" asked Clark.

"Even with the aliens," said Bakker.

"I don't understand what happened," he said. "That's not the way it is."

"No," said Bakker, "but it's the way it is here, on this Earth."

"I don't get it."

"This is not the Earth of our reality, but another Earth in another universe where the aliens found us and took over the planet."

"So that's what we've been doing all the time?" asked

Hackett. "Traveling between, or rather, among these different realities?"

"Yes."

Thinking about it, he said, "Then we saw a reality where the dinosaurs survived, and one where animal life didn't evolve, and now this one where the aliens we met at the edge of the Solar System diverted to take a look at us rather than pass by on their original mission."

"Yes. Or came back to take a look."

Hackett laughed and said, "I don't know what good this has done us."

"It expanded our universe beyond the one we knew and lets us roam through the others."

"To what benefit?" asked Clark.

"Think about it. What has been the purpose of our explorations throughout the galaxy? To preserve the human race and to find new places for us to colonize. We found one very nice world with no animal life to complicate the process. We found another where there seemed to be no intelligent life, but abundant animal life. There must be millions of those worlds. And millions of worlds where the aliens didn't land and millions where there were no Dark Ages and so on and so on."

Clark snorted and said, "But it's not the same as colonization of the galaxy we know."

Hackett understood but asked, "Why not?"

"Because travel into another universe isn't possible," said Clark. "Because there aren't these multi-universes. There is only one reality."

Bakker waved a hand. "But there are others. You're standing in one now."

"Yes, but—"

"No buts about it," said Bakker. "Travel between them or among them was impossible until recently, but then travel to the stars was impossible until a couple of hundred years ago. We found a doorway out of our universe and into others, and now we can make all the universes into one reality."

Hackett laughed and grinning, said, "We'll have to change the name from the Galaxy Exploration Team to the Universe Exploration Team."

Bakker looked at him and said, "And think what we can learn. Assuming an infinite number of universes, every problem will have been encountered and solved—"

"How do you know?" asked Clark.

"Because there are an infinite number of possibilities. There'll be an Earth where they had the atomic war and one where there was no Dark Ages and one where the glaciers didn't retreat and one where Jupiter ignited as another star and every other possibility. We can search those realities to find the best solutions for our problems and adopt them."

Hackett suddenly felt the blood drain from his face, felt weak in the knees, and slightly sick. They had just found the gate to the universe . . . all the universes.

He looked at Bakker and said, "How do we know that we're the first to do this?"

"It doesn't matter now that we know."

EPILOGUE

[1]

O'NEILL SAT IN A COMFORTABLE CHAIR AND
looked across the open space, where a holographic display
would manifest if there was one, and saw that Pierce was
staring at him. The look on Pierce's face was not a pleasant one. It seemed that Pierce was blaming O'Neill for the
failure of the project, but O'Neill didn't believe the project
had failed.

Travis and Griffin entered and sat down. A moment
later, the holograph display opened up and Anderson
Thomas was sitting there, in a slowly rotating chair about
two feet above the floor. He was able to look into the faces
of each of the participants, though not all at once.

"O'Neill," he said.

O'Neill felt himself grow cold. He didn't know what he
was going to say. Suddenly he did feel like he had failed.

"Yes?"

"Tell me what you have."

O'Neill looked up and saw the back of Thomas's head. He waited until the rotation brought Thomas back around and said, "We have found ourselves not traveling among the stars as we thought, but among various universes."

"I know that. What do you have?"

Travis said, "Sir, Mr. O'Neill was not fully aware of the reasons for our explorations until recently. He didn't know about Nemesis or the threat to the inner planets."

"But now he does?"

"Of course. We have briefed him fully now that a solution is in place."

"So," said Thomas, "What do you have for me?"

"Apparently, and we have now confirmed this to our satisfaction, we are opening a portal, or gate, between our reality and others, using the device we call the fish tank. We are able to travel to other realities, other universes, with relative ease and with little danger to us and with virtually no expenditure of resources other than electrical."

"And this is significant to me how?" asked Thomas rather snottily.

"My mission, as I now understand it," said O'Neill, "was to provide a haven against Nemesis. If the close approach caused objects in both the Kuiper belt and the Oort cloud to invade the inner planets, we wanted to ensure the survival of humanity. If people are not here, regardless of where they are, then we have accomplished that mission. Once the danger has passed, they can return."

"My thinking," said Thomas waving an expansive hand, "was to populate the stars."

O'Neill nodded and said, "But if that was the only goal,

then faster-than-light travel, hell, even the Generation Ships, accomplished that."

"I wanted to establish two-way communications. I want to be able to protect humanity from Nemesis and return them to their home world."

"We can accomplish that now," said O'Neill, suddenly feeling better. "We can protect humanity."

Clinton spoke up then. "We have an added benefit. There are unlimited possibilities here. Each universe differs from ours. Some dramatically, such as the one where the dinosaurs evolved into an intelligent race building a civilization. Others are only slightly different. They have faced problems and solved them. We can explore them and learn those solutions."

"You mean pirate them," said Thomas.

"That's not what I had in mind," said Clinton angrily. "I meant that we wouldn't have to waste time searching for a solution. Just take the best."

"How reliable is this gate of yours?" asked Thomas.

"We log the settings used to open the gate and push the fish tank through. If we use the same settings each time, along with the same power input, then we find the same world. We think of the setting as the specific address. If we vary it at all, even one setting out of the dozen we need, we find a new and different world."

Thomas interrupted again. "You are telling me that we have a solution to the immediate problem."

"Yes. And I'm telling you that we can explore a thousand other worlds to find the best solution for us. Humanity will survive, and we will expand throughout the galaxy."

O'Neill laughed. "We might not be able to easily communicate, but we will fill the galaxy."

Thomas smiled for the first time since the meeting began. He said, "I started this project to ensure survival, knowing that Nemesis is out there. Now you tell me that finally, we have the stars. We have them for real."

"That's exactly what I'm saying.

"Then I declare this meeting over."

[2]

HACKETT SAT IN HIS OFFICE AND STUDIED THE parade of images on his flat-screen. They were in full color, often with accompanying odors, and certainly with stereo sound.

Bakker sat in one of the chairs, watching as well. Finally she said, "They knew about Nemesis and didn't say a thing to us. Just threw us out there."

Hackett turned his attention to her and said, "It is a philosophical question. You know of the possibility of the end of civilization, and believe that the major catastrophe will come in about a hundred years, so do you say anything? How could we have prepared?"

"But they were planning for it. Why not seek the help of everyone? Who knows what might have happened?"

"Precisely," said Hackett. "Remember what happened when we announced, simply, that another intelligence had been found. Riot and panic."

"Yes, but that didn't start until we learned their spacecraft was coming toward us. And, more importantly, until the media and the politicians began milking the story for their own personal gain."

"The point you're missing," said Hackett, "is that people, without waiting to learn all they could, went nuts."

Bakker grinned at that. "Precise scientific language."

"I notice that you don't contradict me."

"You know what I find interesting about all this? We still haven't found a good way to travel interstellar distances. We have faster-than-light, but that sets up problems for the astronauts. We have the Generation Ships, but that means the colonists are never going to return. And our gate allows us into other realities, but we still aren't traveling interstellar distances with any kind of success."

"But the real achievement," said Hackett, "is that we have pushed humanity out of the Solar System. If the sun goes nova, humanity will survive. If Nemesis does bombard the inner planets, humanity will survive. We have begun the process of colonizing the galaxy. Something that I didn't expect to see in my lifetime."

"It has been a long one," said Bakker. "I mean, who'd have thought you'd be around more than two hundred years after your birth."

"Yeah. And who'd have thought that I would travel to the stars, to other realities, and be happiest living on Mars?"

"So what do we do now?" asked Bakker.

"Retire, I think. I've had enough exploring the galaxy in its many forms. You?"

"The same." She crossed over him and took his hand. "Let's go home."

The Exploration Chronicles
by Kevin D. Randle

Book One: SIGNALS
0-441-01039-3

In New Mexico, devices monitoring the desert skies pick up faint but unmistakable sounds: signals coming from a mere fifty light years away and headed toward Earth. But will the approaching beings be friendly? As Earth struggles towards a unified response, one thing becomes clear—we are about to meet our neighbors.

Book Two: STARSHIP
0-441-01128-4

Starship Alpha is a "generation ship" on an interstellar journey to locate the souce of the extraterrestrial signals first heard on Earth over two hundred years ago. Now, as new generations born aboard the ship threaten to abandon the mission, humanity's destiny lies in the hands of one boy.

Book Three: F.T.L.
0-441-01192-6

First there were signs of alien life in *Signals*. Then *Starship* launched the tale of humanity's next step toward the stars. Now, in *F.T.L.*, the quest for faster-than-light travel begins.